PRAISE FOR
MY BROTHER'S KEEPER

From the opening words of Bill Kassel's novel, we are drawn into the complex and colorful world of first-century Palestine. The reader is caught up in the drama of Christ through the eyes of Jesus' natural family. Kassel's work is unconventional, exciting and even controversial, offering fresh insight and inspiration for believers and non-believers alike.

Fr. Dwight Longenecker
Author, *The Romance of Religion*

Kassel moves into legal thriller territory with the famous trial before Pilate. Engaging, original, and provocative, this one's a keeper.

John Lescroart
New York Times Bestselling Author

Bill Kassel has taken a very different approach to the Christian story. His is not the conventional Christmas card portrait of the Holy Family. Rather, he has delved deeply into the earliest writings in Church Tradition, and offered some compelling suppositions about what was going on around Jesus and how the people closest to him might have been affected by it.

Fr. Joe Krupp
Faith Magazine

Joseph is convinced that Mary's boy has a special destiny, which he fears will place Jesus in danger. On his deathbed, Joseph pleads with his own son, James (whom the Bible calls "the brother of the Lord"), to protect Jesus .... The novel makes one think, unlike some novels nowadays. It's a way of introducing the Gospel to non-Christians—which is what we're supposed to be doing.

Nancy Hastings
Gatehouse Media Group

Continued...

Using James, the brother of the Lord, to anchor his story, Kassel tries to fill in the gaps of the Gospels regarding the life of Jesus. Through pious tradition and information garnered from the Apocryphal Gospels, Kassel provides a remarkably orthodox tale covering things that have challenged the Christian imagination over millennia. Kassel's appreciation of the Jewishness of Jesus is enhanced by his research into Judaism's laws and customs. His command of the history of the period makes his book both instructive and engaging. This literary genre goes back to at least the second century, but Kassel gives it a contemporary plausibility readers will appreciate.

Fr. Michael P. Orsi
Contributor, *Homiletic and Pastoral Review*

My Brother's Keeper is a book of history, and, yes, entertainment. Even though we all know how it will end, I can't put it down! It's one of those stories you find yourself thinking of when you go about your daily routine .... Whether you are a Christian or not, this is an awesome read.

Nancy Ryan
Book Reviewer, *Simply Hers Magazine*

In every family there exists someone who is definitely a little different, someone who says or believes things others dare not say or perhaps never pondered. It is quite another thing when something that person said actually comes true and miracles are performed. What must have been the word on the street or village, and what must those who were close to Jesus and his family thought? Bill Kassel takes you there. Take a step back in time, and imagine how you would have thought had you lived in Israel some 2,000 years ago, dealing with the harsh reality of daily life in the cruel world of the Roman-occupied Middle East. When you heard stories of Jesus of Nazareth, would you have been a believer?

Dave Hartline
Contributor, *American Catholic*

I found it very interesting that the author chose to incorporate early Christian traditions held by both Catholicism and Orthodoxy .... The character on which the novel focuses is James, the half-brother of Jesus, known as "James the Just," who throughout the novel evolves from a knowledge-hungry young man to a very respected rabbi and the Jewish advisor of Pontius Pilate .... The author did a fantastic job exploring the motivations that drove Pilate to condemn Jesus to death although knowing He was innocent. The plot leading up to the Passion story is presented with great depth and reverence, meant to incite further discussion of what led to the sacrifice of Jesus and what its implications, whether political, social or spiritual, were.

Alex Szollo
International Book Reviewer, Romania

One might expect that, since anyone who has read the Bible knows how that story ends, there would be little incentive to keep turning the pages. For this reader, at least, the book was hard to put down. It's a tribute to the skill of the author that the characters are so believable and robust that one becomes emotionally involved with them. Although the events are set two thousand years in the past, there is an almost modern feel to the narrative. The complex characters, both public and domestic, could have stepped out of our lives, and the horror and cruelty of political repression are all too familiar in our time.

Diane Osbourne
Contributor, *Stubborn Things*

If I had lived in the time of Jesus, who would I think He was? What would I have believed about Him? Would I have espoused His teachings? It wasn't like being raised Christian in the 20th century. My Brother's Keeper made me realize in a fresh new way how hard it was, in Jesus' time, for many people—especially Jews—to believe in Jesus, and how amazing His mission really was.

Cheryl Nael
Ave Maria Radio

Continued...

Kassel has created a vivid landscape for his characters that can be clearly seen felt and almost touched. The interaction between the characters is understated and dutiful, with silent respect. The reader can almost hear their thoughts in humble reverential tones. The relationships come across as genuine, the narrative moves along smoothly, and the storyline in engaging. All in all, a very good read.

Al Ferber
Poet & Author

My Brother's Keeper was, for me, a most gratifying reading experience. The book is beautifully written. And even with my limited early Christian history knowledge, I could tell that it had been exhaustively researched. I consider it a significant literary achievement. It was a privilege to read it.

Gordon Boardman
Artist & Writer

What kind of sibling rivalry exists when one of the children is the Son of God? How do you educate him when he is the Wisdom of God? He created the universe, but how does he learn to work with his hands? Kassel elaborates, adapts and embroiders, but never contradicts the biblical material. In the process he spins a yarn of intrigue and adventure that sets the protagonist—James, "the brother of the Lord"—struggling mightily (if mistakenly) to save Jesus from the gruesome death which we now know was the will of God all along ... My Brother's Keeper is a creative and stimulating form of meditation that entertains like a novel but edifies like a prayer. It's part of a vibrant movement by a new wave of serious Christian novelists to sustain (or perhaps, rebuild?) a Catholic educational/literary culture that has long been a key underpinning of our Judeo-Christian civilization.

Al Kresta
Catholic Radio Pioneer
Host of "Kresta In the Afternoon"
(1951-2024)

MY BROTHER'S KEEPER

A NOVEL ABOUT THE FAMILY OF JESUS
PART I
THE STORY OF A BIRTH

BILL KASSEL

EMPEROR BOOKS

MY BROTHER'S KEEPER

Published by Emperor Books

Bellerose Village, NY

ISBN

Digital 978-1-63777-672-8

Print 978-1-63777-673-5

Cover Image: "The Nativity" by Fra Filippo Lippi (c1445), Courtesy National Gallery of Art, Washington, DC.

Map "Palestine in the Time of Jesus" by Charles Foster Kent (1867-1925), Courtesy Library of Congress

Hebrew characters on title page spell out the phrase "my brother's keeper."

CONTENTS

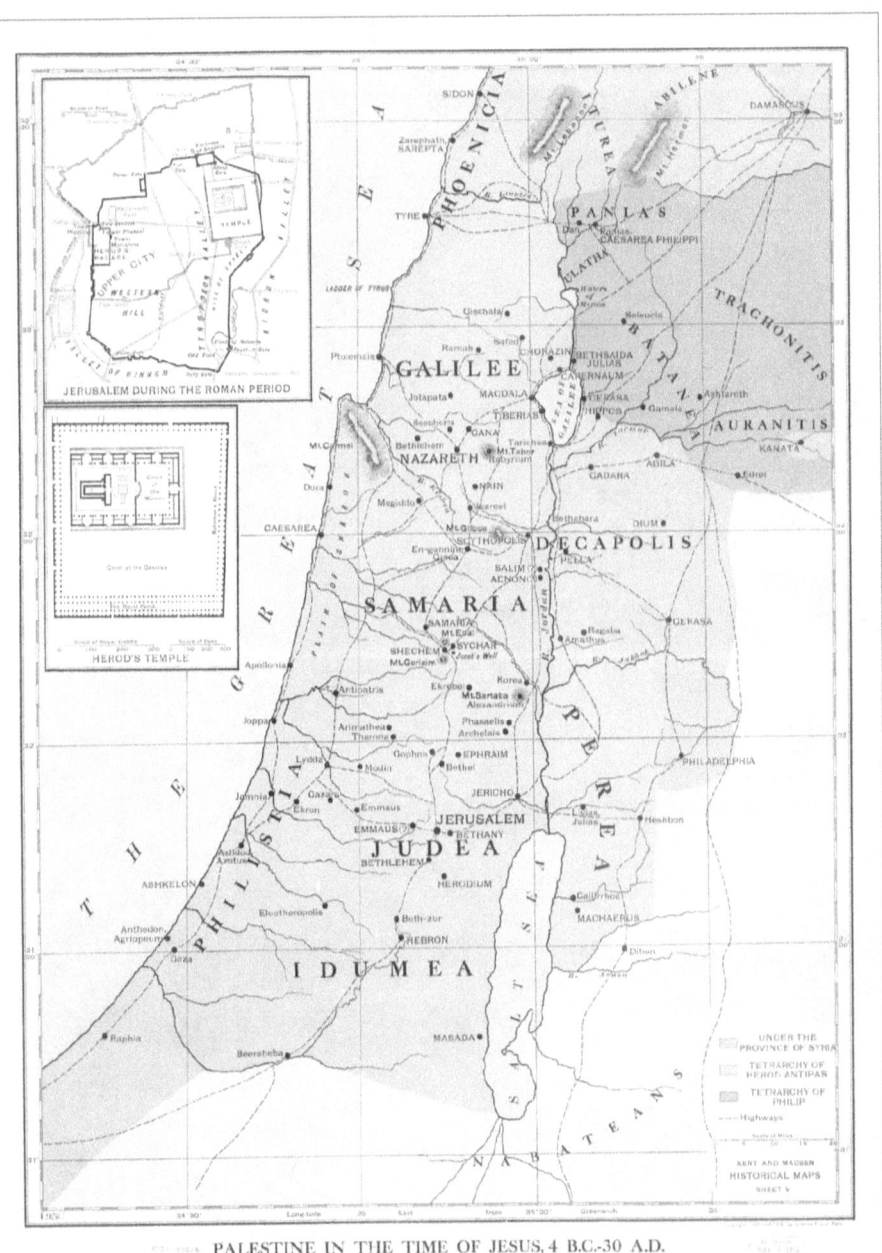

JERUSALEM DURING THE ROMAN PERIOD

HEROD'S TEMPLE

SIDON

Zarephath,
SAREPTA

PHOENICIA

ITUREA

ABILENE

DAMASCUS

TYRE

PANIAS

Dan, Kadesh

CAESAREA PHILIPPI

GAULANITIS

TRACHONITIS

LADDER OF TYRUS

Gischala

Phoenicia

Ramah

Safed

CHORAZIN

BETHSAIDA
JULIAS

BATANEA

GALILEE

Jotapata

MAGDALA

CAPERNAUM

Seleucia

AURANITIS

Sepphoris

CANA

TIBERIAS

SEA OF
GALILEE

Gamala

KANATA

Mt.Carmel

Bethlehem

Mt.Tabor

Tarichaea

HIPPOS

Edrei

NAZARETH

Dora

Megiddo

NAIN

Endor

GADARA

ABILA

DIUM

CAESAREA

SCYTHOPOLIS

Hethabara

DECAPOLIS

Engannim
Ginaea

PELLA

SALIM?
AENON?

GERASA

SAMARIA

SAMARIA
Mt.Ebal

SHECHEM
Mt.Gerizim

SYCHAR
Jacob's Well

Ragaba

Amathus

Apollonia

Antipatris

Ekrebel

Mt.Sartaba
Alexandrium

Korea

PEREA

Arimathea
Thamna

Phaenelis

Archelais

Gophna

EPHRAIM

Joppa

Lydda

Modin

Bethel

PHILADELPHIA

Jamnia

Gaza

JERICHO

Emmaus

Livias
Julias

Heshbon

Ekron

EMMAUS?

JERUSALEM

BETHANY

JUDEA

BETHLEHEM

HERODIUM

ASHKELON

Eleutheropolis

Beth-zur

Callirrhoe

MACHAERUS

Anthedon-
Agrippeum

HEBRON

Dibon

Gaza

IDUMEA

PHILISTIA

Raphia

Beersheba

MASADA

NABATEANS

UNDER THE
PROVINCE OF SYRIA

TETRARCHY OF
HEROD ANTIPAS

TETRARCHY OF
PHILIP

Highways

KENT AND MADDEN
HISTORICAL MAPS
SHEET V

PALESTINE IN THE TIME OF JESUS, 4 B.C.-30 A.D.
(INCLUDING THE PERIOD OF HEROD, 40-4 B.C.)

Out of Zion the law shall go forth,
and the word of the Lord from Jerusalem.
(Isaiah 2)

PROLOGUE
FAMILY BEGINNINGS

T he house of Joseph was located at the northern edge of the town on a grassy hill. There Avram the shepherd, of blessed memory, had once kept a sheepfold in which he would pen his animals until they were shorn or selected out for sale to Nathan, the butcher.

When Avram had owned the hill, before Joseph came from Bethlehem of Judea, the knoll was thought of as outside the town, half a Sabbath journey beyond the last house on the street. But Nazareth had grown. Being close to the great city of Sepphoris, it had prospered from work provided to craftsmen in the surrounding country by the Greek merchants eager to enlarge their villas, as well as by the legion command for construction of new billets for Roman troops in transit and the storage and distribution houses that supplied posts and garrisons throughout Galilee.

By the time Joseph came to Nazareth with his wife, Escha, new dwellings had already shortened the road up from town, and Avram the shepherd had recently died.

Having no children, Avram's widow sold the land to this young carpenter and builder, and then went to the home of a kinsman to spend her own last days.

Joseph and Escha moved into the small limestone hut in which Avram had kept his fodder and sheltered himself against the rain. A new roof and door made the place habitable enough, but Joseph's building skills soon yielded another room, in which their first son, Josis, was born. That was followed by an upper chamber on the new section, accessible by a stairway running up the outside to a door at the top sheltered by a wooden enclosure. The original hut was given over completely to the purpose of a shop where Joseph daily plied his woodworking trade. A wall, built of the same limestone plentiful in the region, came next, enclosing a court with its own well, a small flock of chickens, and a she-goat.

The family grew—to five children, before long—in tandem with Joseph's spreading reputation as a man of superior craft, industriousness and reliability. As the years passed, he found himself spending less time fashioning carefully wrought wood furniture and household implements for the people of Nazareth, and more adding to the growing array of fine houses and public structures in Sepphoris.

Indeed, Joseph and his crews of workers were highly praised among the city residents, whom the Jews called Greeks whether they be Roman or any of the other nationalities represented among the foreign intruders. And if his neighbors in Nazareth felt some unease about Joseph's many dealings with pagans, feelings were soothed by the pagan gold he brought back to town. As the old expression went, "A workman deserves his wage," and it was Joseph who came to provide so much of it.

While he might not be considered a man of wealth to the measure of his Greek patrons, Joseph was a man of accomplishment. And with his indisputable piety—faithful in attendance at synagogue and study of Torah, despite so many demands of business upon his time—he was respected, someone to be turned to in trust.

Joseph and Escha lived in as much hopefulness and serenity as could be expected in a land under the control of a usurper king backed by a foreign force. Indeed, while Nazareth was close to the great imperial enclave of Sepphoris, it was much less touched by the intrigues and strife of Jerusalem, to which Bethlehem was located so near. A certain kind of peace prevailed here in the hills of Galilee.

And so it was in this sedate household that Joseph and Escha raised three sons and two daughters. Josis, the eldest, trained at his father's side, mastering carpentry skills and joining Joseph in the family business. Judas and Simon, being more drawn to country pursuits, brought sheep back to old Avram's grassy hill, their sheepfold abutting the outer side of the court wall. They also secured some seedlings of olive trees with the intention of establishing a grove.

All three of the sons took wives, and the wall became pierced with doorways into new dwellings built in a cluster, so that the house of Joseph grew into a compound of some size. Marriages were arranged for Lydia and Assia, the daughters, who thus made their homes with their husbands in the town. Grandchildren abounded on old Avram's hill, the boys learning to assist their fathers in the trades of the household, and the girls learning womanly skills at their mothers' sides.

And then, in the fullness of her days, Escha conceived unexpectedly and gave birth to a fourth son, James. But the joy of this late blessing was dampened by a sudden turn in her health. Escha's healing was not proper, and she was never fully strong after that birth. She collapsed on the morning of the child's circumcision, and had to be carried to her bed.

No one could say if her illness had been caused by James' birth. She vomited, passed blood, and ate less and less as painful weeks wore on. Lydia and Assia came from their homes every day to help their brothers' wives in caring for the baby and attending their mother, but to no avail. Joseph was heartsick to see her wasting in such a manner.

Finally, one day Escha pulled her husband close and whispered a few labored words. "This little James is the child of your old age," she said with great difficulty. "He is the last of me. He is what I leave to you, my husband. And you must love him like Jacob loved his favorite son. Promise me that you will not charge this child with my loss, and that you will love him always."

With tears in his eyes, Joseph took his wife's chilled and weakened fingers between calloused hands that were strong but now shaking from his great sadness and fear. "I will love him," he told her. "I will cherish this boy, and make him a great scholar and a man who is held in high regard. This I promise you, my wife."

Escha smiled and turned her face away to sleep. And by the time night had come upon the house of Joseph, she was dead.

PART ONE
UNDER HEROD

CHAPTER ONE

A STRANGE REQUEST

Whoever pursues righteousness and kindness will find life and honor.
(Proverbs 21)

The Rabbi Ezra surveyed the small cluster of students, only four today. They sat on rough wooden benches in the mottled shade of an overhead screen of olive branches woven into a loose wicker. The crude shelter, set in the court that separated the rabbi's house from Nazareth's small synagogue, served as a classroom in pleasant weather. It did double duty as a harvest hut for the rabbi and his wife during the annual feast of booths.

He chose a random psalm to check his students' memorization. *The earth is the Lord's and all its bounty...*he began, leaving the line incomplete. The boys dutifully picked up from him—*the world and all who dwell in it*—reciting through to the end with only occasional stumbles among some of them.

"Better," said the rabbi, "better." Then he pointed at a small boy, the newest member of the class, just five years old. "And who is the King of Glory, Abner son of Benjamin? I don't think I quite heard you say it."

The little boy was startled at first and searched his memory. Then he recalled that he knew perfectly well who the King of Glory was. "The Lord of Hosts is the King of Glory, Master," he said assertively.

"Yes," said the rabbi, smiling broadly. "The Lord of Hosts is the King of Glory. Very good, Abner son of Benjamin."

All the boys laughed.

Ezra straightened in his seat and gestured in the direction of the oldest boy. "Yesterday we heard the story of Cain and Abel," he said, "which was read to us very nicely by James son of Joseph." At this mention, James turned his eyes down into his lap self-consciously. He often felt slightly embarrassed when the rabbi complimented him. Ezra made it a point to praise all his students, believing kind words a better encouragement to learning than the harsh criticism, even scorn, on which some teachers relied. Still, James often sensed that the rabbi was the merest bit quicker to recognize his accomplishments than those of his fellows. There was a reason for that, and it made him somewhat uncomfortable.

It was well known to those familiar with the family of Joseph the builder that James held a special place in his father's heart. But no one ever observed any resentment expressed toward him by his brothers or sisters. Indeed, it had often been remarked that Joseph avoided the error of their forefather, Jacob, who as Scripture recounted, doted on his favored child in ways that sowed seeds of bitterness.

There was a certain sweet honesty about James that endeared him to the adults in the family and made him a hero to the household children. Because of his scholarly bent and the diligence he brought to his studies, no one ever begrudged the time he spent in ceaseless questioning of the Rabbi Ezra or pious reflection on the holy books, even when it took him from chores in the compound.

That James would one day be a doctor of the Law was an assumption shared by all, especially Ezra. The rabbi was always willing to invest time in the boy, over and above the hours spent in class. This was partly due to his recognition of James' abilities, and partly out of gratitude for some extra support provided by James' father.

Nazareth being a small town based principally on its surrounding farms and herds, Ezra's students were often called upon to work in the fields and so could not be counted on for regular attendance in class. This made the stipends on which Ezra depended somewhat erratic. Since Joseph was deeply concerned for the continuity of his son's schooling, he had a quiet understanding with the rabbi to make up the difference whenever students were away and Ezra's earnings fell short. It kept things going, regardless of how many students were present.

The supplement was invaluable and much appreciated by a humble scholar with few opportunities for added income. To Joseph it was a practical arrangement by which he expected no privileges for his son beyond the privilege of learning. Still, Ezra couldn't help but feel a special stake in this particular student. James was aware of that, and so often wondered if a certain amount of this rabbinical attention might be more than was deserved by his actual scholarly gifts, ample though they were.

"What did all of you think about this story?" Ezra asked the class. The group was silent. James, too, said nothing. He knew the day's lesson was aimed at the younger boys, and the rabbi did not expect him to respond.

Ezra waited. Then: "Well, let us recall what happened in the story. Ephraim son of Joel, what did the two brothers do?"

The chubby boy, son of the town blacksmith, wrinkled up his face in thought. "They made sacrifice to the Lord," he said after a moment. "That's right," Ezra said. "And what did they bring before the Lord?"

Ephraim thought again. "Well..." he said, "Cain brought crops, and..." His words dissolved into the silence of uncertainty.

"Yes, Cain was a tiller of the fields," the rabbi said. "And what was Abel?"

The strain of remembering was apparent in the boy's soft features, but all his effort yielded no result.

Ezra turned to another student. "Caleb son of Mathias, do you remember what was the work of Abel?"

"He was a shepherd," the boy answered quickly with a grin at his triumph over a classmate.

"A shepherd, yes," the rabbi said. "And what would a shepherd offer as a sacrifice?"

"He offered a lamb," said Caleb.

The rabbi clapped his hands together. "A lamb," he said, glancing at James, who was amused at the rabbi's playful and teacherly prompting.

"Now," said Ezra, "what happened when Cain and Abel made sacrifice? Was the Holy One pleased?" He pointed to Abner. "Abner son of Benjamin, did the Lord like what Cain and Abel brought Him?" The boy hesitated. "Y—yes...?" he proposed warily.

"Did He?" asked the rabbi. "Remember the story which James son of Joseph read to us."

Caleb waved a hand to attract his teacher's attention. "The Lord liked Abel's gift," he said.

"Ah! Caleb son of Mathias recalls that the lamb of Abel was pleasing to the Holy One," said Ezra. "But what of the crops brought by Cain?"

"He didn't like them," said Ephraim, at last connecting with yesterday's reading.

"You're right, He didn't like them. And how did this make Cain feel?"

Caleb was about to speak again, but the rabbi looked at the boy, winked, and held a finger to his lips. Caleb smiled in satisfaction, understanding that his teacher realized he knew the answer.

"Ephraim son of Joel, Abner son of Benjamin, how did Cain feel?" asked Ezra.

"He felt bad," said Ephraim.

"Yes." The rabbi nodded his head solemnly. "He felt very bad. In fact, the story tells us that Cain's face fell." The rabbi's features became an exaggerated mask of comic sadness at which everyone laughed.

In such a back-and-forth manner, Ezra led the group through a recounting of Abel's murder at the hands of his brother and the Lord's banishment of Cain. He emphasized the seriousness of Cain's act, but took care not to present the tale in a way that was too frightening to the children whose minds it was his duty to nurture.

When the lesson was concluded, James lingered in the wicker-shaded enclosure. It was not unusual for him to remain behind to ask some question of his teacher or discuss the day's topic in more detail than would have interested the other students, even those closer to his own age. But today he sat quietly, gazing off in the direction of the synagogue building.

Ezra noted the boy's distraction. "Something burdens your mind, James son of Joseph?"

James turned to his teacher. "Oh...no, Master," he said. "Not really. It's just that... Well, I have heard the story of Cain and Abel so many times, and..."

"Yes?"

"Rabbi, I have never understood why the Holy One should have rejected Cain's offering. Didn't Cain bring what he had to give, just as his brother did?"

"Do you think the Lord was unfair to Cain?"

"It seems like He favored Abel. And I don't know why."

Ezra sat down on the bench next to the boy. "This is a question the sages have pondered," he said. "Some note that the scriptures mention particularly that Abel offered the finest of his flock—where it's merely recorded that Cain offered crops, with no description of what they were or how good they might have been. So perhaps Cain was holding back his best and he deserved the Lord's rebuke."

"But we don't know that."

"This is true. We don't know."

"What if he did pick the best of his crops to give?"

"Mmm... He might have. But even if he did, there could be a problem in that also."

"How?"

Ezra seized upon an opportunity to push the boy into deeper reflection. "Well," he said, "here you must try to think like the sages who understand that Scripture teaches as much by what it doesn't say as by what it does. Suppose Cain had worked very hard, day in and day out, in all kinds of weather to make things grow, and then he chose very carefully so that he would be sure to set only his very best produce before the Holy One of Israel. And maybe, through all those days when he was toiling in the field, he had watched his brother lounging with his flock or leading the animals aimlessly about. Maybe all of this had made Cain feel that his efforts were better than those of Abel. Could it be the Lord saw that Cain was puffed up with his own superiority? Perhaps the Holy One knew that Cain had come to despise his brother even before the two made their offerings."

James examined the situation posed by Ezra. "My brothers are shepherds," he said. "They are farmers, too, if you think about the olive grove they're trying to make."

"At which tasks do they work harder?" the rabbi asked.

"I'm not sure," James said. "With the olive trees they must dig and fertilize and water. With the sheep they must haul feed, and of course they have to sheer them. All of that is work."

"Yes. All of that is work," Ezra agreed. "So I guess we cannot really know what was in Cain's heart, and we cannot be sure why Abel's gift was pleasing to the Lord and Cain's not."

"Then what can we learn from the story, Rabbi?" James asked.

Ezra saw the boy's puzzled expression, and he smiled in a kindly way that was intended to encourage. "Perhaps what we can learn," he said, "is that the Lord has His own designs."

This time of year, classes were dismissed before the day's heat accumulated fully, so it was still morning when James arrived back at the family compound. He performed the usual entrance ritual, kissing his fingers and touching the scroll of the Commandment (called in Hebrew a *mezuzah*), the small piece of parchment bearing Torah verses and rolled inside a niche in the doorpost. He noticed that there were no children in sight, which struck him as unusual, since the court was normally alive with the din of childish play.

There were, however, two men standing in the portico of the house he shared with his father, who was at this moment addressing them, head slightly bowed in humble greeting. Approaching the portico, James recognized one of the visitors: Joachim, an aged neighbor and the wealthiest man in Nazareth, holder of vast estates on which perhaps a fifth of the farmers in the region were tenants. James' brothers, Judas and Simon, pastured their flock on part of his land. The other visitor was a stranger, and an especially distinguished looking one. Though clearly older than James' father, this man stood imposingly to the full extent of his tall size. His robes and turban were bleached a bright white, and the sash around his middle was an interlacing of cords in different colors woven with flecks of gold. James recognized it as a badge of status.

Joseph spotted his son, and made a gesture which the boy caught and understood. James ran to the side of the house, found a basin and sponge, and went to the well in the court. He filled the basin with water, and brought it to the portico. Joseph motioned the visitors to be seated, and they placed themselves side-by-side on a wooden bench whose edges were carved in a motif of vines and leaves. Joachim exhibited some slight difficulty in doing so.

The boy knelt down, removed their sandals, and proceeded to wash their feet with the sponge. Their nodding heads acknowledged the gesture of hospitality.

"My son, James," said Joseph, taking a stool and seating himself across from the visitors.

Joachim eyed the boy approvingly. "He has grown," the old man said. "What age is he now?"

"Soon to be twelve years," Joseph replied.

"So he will celebrate his maturity in just over a year then?" Joseph nodded. "He looks forward to when he can be counted as one of the ten men for a service."

"Wonderful," said the tall, distinguished-looking visitor. "A fine son."

James completed the foot washing, stood with the basin, and bowed. He would not presume to refasten the guests' sandals. Joseph put a hand on the boy's shoulder. "James," he said, "you know our esteemed townsman, Master Joachim."

It wasn't the most common thing for a young boy to be included in introductions among adults, but the warmth between father and son was evident to the visitors. James bowed toward Joachim, holding his tongue as befit his youth.

"But I especially wish for you to remember the day," Joseph continued, "when you were in the presence of the honored Zacharias, great priest of the Lord's temple."

James emitted a quick gasp, and his eyes went immediately to the tall man. The boy was duly impressed, as his father had known he would be. For such a figure to grace Joseph's home was an occasion to be spoken of down the generations.

Joachim smiled, amused at the boy's stunned reaction. "James studies the holy books with great diligence," he said to his companion. "Is that not true, Joseph?"

"My son has been a student of the Rabbi Ezra, here in Nazareth, since the age of five years. Ezra tells me that James has great prospects. He often has him lead the other boys in their recitations. When he is older, Ezra will find him a more learned master."

Zacharias smiled kindly at the boy. "A joy to you, Joseph, I am sure," he said. "But he should learn in Jerusalem. When the time comes, send him to me. I will see to a placement in one of the houses of study."

Joseph glanced at James and met the boy's eyes. Then he looked back at the exalted visitor. "I...would be forever grateful," Joseph said, unsure at what should prompt such a statement. Was it a sincere offer, or merely a social nicety?

James' face was reddened from the kind words spoken about him. He withdrew from the porch, carrying the basin.

The unsparing Galilean sun had brought the court near to its usual, cooking, midday temperature. But a slight breeze left Joseph and his guests cool in the shade of the portico. The two visitors sat quietly for a while, leaving their host in great perplexity about the reason for their coming. James shared his father's curiosity, though he shared it at a distance, listening from behind a large bush at the end of the portico by the stairway leading to the upper room.

Joachim appeared to Joseph to be somewhat unsettled, which could have been the effect of his poor health. He was indeed quite aged, his hands had a noticeable tremor, his skin was pale with many flaked patches, and the shock of fine, pure-white hair sticking almost straight out from under his cap was buffeted easily by even the slightest movement of the air. Joseph noted that he seemed as uncomfortable sitting as he had when he was shuffling slowly across the court. The old man had suffered the loss of his wife, Anna, not more than two years before, and it was said in the town that her passing had accelerated his long decline.

Joachim looked around the court, and then turned this gaze up to the sheltering roof overhead. "When you added this structure," he said, "it was just before the wedding of your son, was it not? What is his name?"

"Simon," said Joseph.

"Simon, of course. The flock. Forgive me. My memory..."

"We completed it in time for his wedding feast," said Joseph.

"I attended. I recall that."

"My house was honored by your presence. Simon is a father three times since then."

"Three times?"

"Yes."

"You are blessed."

"The Lord is generous," Joseph said.

"The Lord is generous," Zacharias repeated.

Joseph suddenly felt a flash of guilt. It was common knowledge that the wife of the famous priest had borne him no children, and he hoped that the joy of his own family life was not a reminder of that sadness. Joachim had been in a similar circumstance until late life. Then, a daughter. Joseph was glad he had instructed his sons' wives to keep all the children out of the court while the visitors were present.

Joachim stirred slightly on the bench, his face showing a fleeting grimace. "We have come, Joseph," he said, "I and my friend and honored kinsman, Zacharias—You are aware that my late wife was sister to Zacharias' wife, Elizabeth?"

"I am," said Joseph.

"Yes. Well...we wish to make...a request."

"Anything I am able to grant," Joseph said.

Zacharias laughed—very slightly, but still a laugh. "You are a most gracious man, Joseph. You must wait until you hear our request."

The priest's remark added to Joseph's increasing puzzlement over this visit. To James' as well. What an extraordinary thing that these men should come here. The carpenter had never before met Zacharias, though the holy man's fame had reached to Nazareth, as throughout all of Galilee and Judea. And as for Joachim—he was a neighbor, Joseph had served him with his carpentry skills, and his sons tenanted their flock in the rich man's fields. But to have him seated here was something very unusual.

"Yes," said Joachim. "It is not a small thing that I wish to ask you."

Now Joseph's curiosity was highly aroused. He waited in silence, but with impatience.

"Joseph," said Joachim, "you know that my daughter, Mary, has lived in the temple precincts. I and my wife, Anna, of blessed memory, had passed many years without the joy of children. Then the Holy One saw fit to bestow a gift. And such was our gratitude—and our relief, really..." He looked at Joseph with a sudden sadness of bitter reflection. "I once tried to make sacrifice in the temple, and the priest told me I was unfit because heaven had withheld children from my wife and me. You cannot imagine the shame."

"The shame was upon that priest," said Zacharias firmly. "I can only say that he was not of Abijah, my priestly division."

"I know, my friend, I know," said Joachim. "But that is past. When Mary came to us...after so long and painful a wait...my wife and I felt it must have suited the Lord's purpose in a special way. The child belonged to the King of the Universe. We cherished her for three years... three wonderful years...until she was weaned. That was all we had any right to hold her as our own. We dedicated her to the service of the Holy One, blessed be He."

"That was a great sacrifice," Joseph said. "It must have been very difficult to give her childhood over to the temple."

Joachim's head moved slowly up and down. "Yes. This is true. Difficult. Still, we were confirmed in our decision when we delivered her to the virgins' quarters." He paused, a hand going to his face, thoughtfully fingering his white and tangled beard. "You would have been amazed, Joseph. We expected the child to cry at our parting. Such a thing would have been natural, what a child *would* do. But she waved us away. I remember her little happy smile. It was a strange thing...so very strange. Her legs carried her up the steps as if she were dancing."

His face lit at the memory, and he started to laugh. "To be truthful, I expected that *we* would cry—Anna and me—and embarrass ourselves in front of the party that had come with us to make our presentation. But we did not. We both experienced a most wonderful feeling of consolation. I have never been able to explain it, or to understand how it should have come upon us, or why. Such things are beyond explaining."

Joseph, of course, was aware of the temple virgins and their life of prayer, study, and service. And he had often heard the gibes about how the priests, for all their tithes and temple tax, would not be able to keep the place running without the little girls and old women who knew where the mops and brooms were kept. Mary was the only child from Nazareth whom Joseph was aware served in the temple. But he had known nothing of the circumstances of her going, beyond town gossip. To hear these details from the lips of her father was moving.

To James it was all quite baffling. He had heard that this neighbor girl was serving in the temple, but he found it hard to imagine a childhood spent separated from home and family, so far away in Jerusalem. He could not imagine a young boy in such circumstances, much less a girl.

Zacharias leaned toward Joseph with hands on knees. The priestly turban gave his face, framed by his silvery gray hair and beard, an aspect of authority. "There is a problem now, however," he said.

"Yes," Joachim agreed, "a problem."

"Let us come to the point," the priest said to Joseph's unspoken agreement.

Despite being made privy to Joachim's family story—an interesting tale and a privilege to hear it—Joseph was no closer to understanding why these visitors were here.

Zacharias sensed a subtle impatience in their host. "Mary has reached nearly fourteen years," he went on. "For some time we have expected her to attain her womanhood and for her first flow of blood to begin. It is surprising that this has not happened already, but surely it will soon. This means that her stay in the temple will be concluded because the days of impurity will come. It is customary for the families of temple virgins to arrange marriages for them upon completing the term of service. Being pious and hard-working young women, they make exemplary wives and mothers. But..."

This hesitation prompted Joachim to speak again. "The problem, Joseph," he said, "is that Mary does not wish to marry. She insists upon carrying on with the dedication her mother and I made for her—that is, on remaining a virgin devoted to the Lord—even though there is no place for a girl her age in the temple."

"We can make no provision for her," said Zacharias.

Joseph took on a quizzical look. "As her father," he said, "do you not have the power to insist that she be absolved of this dedication? If you never intended for it to be lifelong, then—"

"Yes, I could do that," said Joachim. "I could do that. But...how can I explain... Mary is an unusual girl, Joseph. Gentle, but...intense. She feels deeply, and she is...insistent." The old man shrugged, his face in a crooked smile. "I am old, Joseph. Perhaps too softhearted? I admit it. I admit it. But I suffer with many infirmities, and I know...that the Lord will call me soon."

"You have kin," Joseph said. "Surely someone could—"

"There are clanship connections through which my properties are entailed," said Joachim. "But Elizabeth, Zacharias' wife, is the only *close* relative."

"We are old, ourselves, you see" said the priest. "One way or the other, Mary would be left alone."

"Even if I had relatives to take her," Joachim said, "how could Mary ever be assured that she could retain her virginity as she wishes? Whoever became her guardian could insist that she marry. I cannot have this, you see. My daughter's welfare must be looked after, her dedication respected. She is so young."

Joseph's curiosity was beginning to give way to unease. What did these men want of him? His three older sons all had wives, and his youngest was but a boy. And in any case, if the girl wished to remain unmarried, what had her commitment to do with him?

Joachim brought his hands together in the lap of his robes, Joseph's eyes following them. They were indeed the hands of an aged one, misshapen, trembling. He saw great pain in the fingers with their swollen joints under almost translucent flesh through which one could clearly discern the outlines of the bones.

"Joseph," said Joachim, now looking away, "it has been quite some years since the passing of your wife, Escha, of blessed memory. Yet, you have not remarried."

Joseph was silent.

"People in the town—I myself, in fact—well...it is often wondered if you might have had opportunities," Joachim said. "Surely, a man of distinction like yourself... You must have been approached. Many families would consider you... That is, the name of Joseph the builder is known throughout the whole of Galilee. You manage workers. You have authority, you have means. Yet you have remained unmarried." He looked directly at Joseph now. "Please, my friend, I know that I have no right to question you in such a way. Forgive me, but..."

"I have a family," said Joseph. "I am in middle life. Actually, a bit *more* than middle life."

"You are younger than I am," said Joachim. "Considerably so."

Joseph nodded. "That is true. And...yes, I have thought about what you suggest. The matchmaker has come to inquire on several occasions. But Escha, my wife... When she died, I just— Well, could another woman find a place in my heart? I don't know. I have never believed so."

"Joseph—if I may..." Joachim was at pains to avoid giving offense, and torn over having to venture into such a private area. Still, he pressed on. "What of a man's...*longing*...my friend? Again, I beg forgiveness. I have no right to question these things, no right at all. And of course, I speak only of the wholesome and proper feelings which a husband has for his wife. But...are such desires...behind you?"

Behind the bush, James' ears perked up, the inquisitiveness of a boy piqued at hearing his father probed along such lines.

Joseph looked from Joachim to Zacharias and then back at Joachim again. He saw no prurience in their faces. Indeed, their eyes bore into him with what was obviously a great sincerity of purpose.

"Surely," he said, "you cannot be thinking of *me* as a match for your daughter. I am well beyond the age even of being her father. I know that such marriages are not uncommon, but I have never thought them wise or fair, especially for the young girls. And besides, if Mary does not want a husband—"

"Mary's wishes are precisely of the essence," Zacharias said. "But...to the question, Joseph—do you no longer feel the needs of a man for a wife?"

Joseph was astonished. He sat quietly for some seconds.

These men had come to ask him to marry Joachim's daughter. He hardly knew how to respond.

"My honored guests," he said at last. "Let me say that I am content with the life which the Lord has given me. He blesses me beyond measure. I am surrounded by my family —children, grandchildren. What more could a man of my age ask? What would be even *right* for him to ask? I have no wish to marry."

"Then, the question of desires..." said Zacharias, not letting the point drop.

Joseph was becoming annoyed. His visitors could see it in his face and in the rigid posture of his body on the stool. He had tried to answer their unwelcome queries in as discreet and dignified a manner as he could.

"Your forbearance and your forgiveness—please," Zacharias insisted. "The question..."

Joseph now felt embarrassment mixed with a feeling that was close to anger. Only his long and high regard for Joachim and the priestly status of Zacharias kept him from being overtaken by temper, something rarely seen in the steady and self-possessed carpenter. "Let my contentment to remain without a wife be an answer to that question," he said. "Draw from it what conclusions you will."

A meaningful glance passed between Joachim and Zacharias, though whatever meaning it contained was quite beyond Joseph. The three men sat silently again for more seconds, Joseph trying to calm himself. Then Joachim, with an exertion that told of his age and weakness, straightened himself on the bench and spoke.

"My friend Joseph, please realize that our presence here, and these intrusive questions, reflect nothing but the utmost respect—which you surely deserve, and which you may be certain we have for you."

"Truly so," Zacharias added.

Again Joseph was without words.

Joachim continued. "My daughter is settled on her virginity. I cannot say that I understand her insistence, and as her father, I do not favor her choice. I would see her wedded to a fine young husband and grandchildren on the way soon after. Such is the outcome I prefer. Still, I respect the strength of her conviction, and I must assume that the hand of the Holy One is in it. Anna and I accepted the sacrifice of our child once, and I am prepared to accept it again. But my time is short, and Mary must be looked after. If a man were prepared to take her into his home—with no expectations that would compromise the discipline she wishes to impose upon herself—such a man would be doing a great kindness, both to Mary and to me."

"It would be a deed of the highest merit," Zacharias added.

Joseph's body lost its stiffness, and he made a long exhalation of breath. As presumptuous and startling as this proposal was, he recognized in it an honor, coming as it did from two men of such high standing.

"She would, of course," Joachim continued, "come with a generous dowry—"

Zacharias interjected, "That is, we do not wish in any way to imply, Joseph—"

"I do not take the words amiss," Joseph said. "Joachim is known to all as someone who is open-handed in the extreme. It is said he gives a generous portion of his income to the temple and its equivalent to the poor. I know he would be most unstinting to any husband, as befits his station and his good name."

"Indeed."

Joseph rose from the stool and walked to the front edge of the portico, standing with his back to Joachim and Zacharias, deep in pondering. James drew farther back around the side of the house to avoid his father's catching him listening in. The visitors glanced at each other again, then at Joseph, waiting for him to turn once more in their direction, which after a time, he did.

"Why do you make this request of *me*, Joachim?" asked Joseph. "We are both of the Tribe of Judah, but surely, that is not reason enough."

Joachim took time before answering the question, choosing his words with deliberation. "I asked myself, Joseph...to what man could I confidently entrust the care of my daughter? I considered several whom I had encountered over the years. Whom did I know that lived his life in accord with the Law of Moses? Who was faithful in fulfilling promises and meeting obligations? Who most had my trust?"

He paused again, stroked his beard, then held out a hand in Joseph's direction. "I have observed you in the execution of your craft and in the affairs of your business. I have seen you deal fairly with those who pay you for work and those who work for you. I have watched you at prayer in the synagogue, heard you read and discuss the holy books. I have observed the fatherly love in which you hold your family. I have sensed prudence, wisdom, charity. I speak here of righteousness, Joseph, *righteousness*. This is what I seek in the man who would care for my precious girl. And so, I come to you."

Joachim's words filled James with pride for his father. But Joseph was shaken. He stood with his eyes closed, almost ashamed to be in the sight of these two men. To hear such a recitation of his merits disturbed him deeply, because it echoed a struggle that had gone on within him all his life. He knew, deep in his heart, that Joachim's description of these qualities was accurate. He had always understood his own virtue. Yet he sought to walk humbly in the way of the Lord. *Humbly.* How can a man be humble when he knows that he is righteous? This was a quandary which Joseph had never been able to resolve.

Without opening his eyes, Joseph said, "It would be a great privilege to have the daughter of Joachim in our family compound." And then he did open his eyes. "We can accommodate her readily," he continued. "My sons and their wives will do their best to make her feel welcome. But marriage...this I do not know. Mary could certainly be regarded as an esteemed guest. A ward, maybe? Some sort of...adoption? Perhaps that would—"

Joachim reacted with a look almost of horror. "No," he said. "That cannot be. For you to adopt Mary while I still live—or for you to take her into your home under such conditions as you mention—this would shame me. People would get wrong, even malicious ideas. It is not without reason that those in other towns repeat the old joke that nothing good comes out of Nazareth. The gossip here can be vicious.

"And an arrangement must be made before I die," he continued. "I fear that Mary would not accept it when I am no longer here to persuade her. My daughter is a young woman of strong will. I must be honest and tell you this, right from the beginning, Joseph. She has a heart large enough to embrace the whole world, but she holds firmly to her own way once an idea has lodged itself in her mind."

"But, of course, this is a strength," Zacharias added quickly. "Mary has great attentiveness and devotion. I have observed it. She learned to weave while living in the temple precincts. She created several panels of the temple veil by herself. Everyone was impressed at her mastery of the craft —the fine work she was able to do, even though she was only a small girl at the time—and at how she persisted in a great and difficult task."

For a moment, Joseph found himself amused at these attempts at persuasiveness on the part of the priest. He knew that Zacharias was a trader when not serving in the temple. His caravans plied the routes to Idumea, Nabatea, the Arabian desert, Damascus, and many other parts far and near. It was obvious that the inclination toward selling did not fail him.

The carpenter returned to his stool and sat, his head turned down. Again, there was silence until, after more uncomfortable seconds, Joachim spoke.

"If you have any thought at all of marrying again, Joseph..." he said, "any at all—I mean to a wife who—" He left the awkward part unmentioned. "Well...I would certainly understand."

"No," Joseph said calmly, "I have no intention of that. In this time of life, my thoughts are not directed toward worldly pleasure. Without Escha...well... You see, I live in the world, and in so many ways, the world has been good to me. But now, my children, my grandchildren, my work— these are all the joy I ask of the world. I have no need of a wife in the way you suggest."

More silence. Joseph leaned forward on his arms, put

his hands to his head, and thought—deeply. He understood that Joachim was a man of pride who would not make such a request as this but for the most tender concern. Joachim loved his daughter, the living sign of the Lord's blessing upon him, the focus of his faith and gratitude. It was hard for Joseph to think of him here in this house near to begging.

Joachim and Zacharias heard a murmuring from Joseph, very quietly, words they could at first barely make out but then recognized as words of prayer: "Blessed are you, Lord our God, King of the Universe..." Joseph's voice trailed off, and all was stillness again. More seconds passed. Finally, the carpenter lifted his head, looked at Joachim, and said, "I will take Mary as my wife under the terms you propose—if she will agree."

Joachim held up his hands as if to clap them together in joy and relief, but then he restrained himself. "Thank you, my good friend," he said, "thank you, thank you. You have made the path to my grave straight and peaceful for me. May your name be remembered throughout the ages."

"You do an important thing this day," Zacharias said. "The Holy One is pleased, blessed be He."

James could see that his father was disturbed in his heart. After returning from the evening service at the synagogue, Joseph had asked Salome, the wife of Josis, to bring him some fruit and bread to eat alone, for there were things on his mind and his hunger was very slight. Salome complied, but included some olives and uncooked vegetables, along with a few pieces of meat, knowing that her husband's father frequently under-judged his appetite.

Josis, Judas, and Simon were at their respective tables, eating with their wives and children. James should have been at Simon's table this night, but he stayed behind, sitting in the shadows at the far corner of the lower room in the lodgings he shared with Joseph. A faint shaft of light, the last of the day, penetrated the open-shuttered window on the west wall, the lamp not yet lit.

James' eyes were on the man who had been his only parent. The boy carried no memory of his mother, since she had died mere weeks after his birth. And while he had been looked after by his sisters and his brothers' wives, his father was the one living soul around whom his life had always turned. Would things be different when the girl, Mary, was in their home? What claims would she make on his father's love and attention? Being young, James only partly understood what he had caught of the discussion about a man's desire for a wife. He had heard Joseph say that he had no such desire, so he assumed his father's marriage would not be quite like that of other men. But what *would* it be like?

And what expectations would the girl have of James? Would she consider herself his new mother? Would Joseph demand that he defer to this stranger who was only two years older than the boy? There were so many questions. Perhaps there were yet no answers. Perhaps that was all part of his father's unsettled mood.

A slight movement of James' foot caused a sound that roused Joseph's attention.

"My son? Are you there?" he asked. "I did not see you. Come out of the dark."

James stood and walked across the room, slipped off his sandals, and deposited himself on a mat near where his father was seated beside a low table.

"Did you eat in Simon's house?" Joseph asked.

"No, Father," said James. "I was not hungry."

"When are you not hungry?"

"Just tonight, Father." And the boy laughed nervously.

"Eat with me," said Joseph. "Salome has brought me more than I need. She always wants to fatten me like a calf."

Father and son washed their hands. Joseph took a small cup, drew water from a basin that sat beside the table and poured it over each of his hands, reciting the prayer for washing. James repeated his father's actions. Then each broke off a piece of the loaf Salome had provided, and recited the blessing of bread. They began picking from a tray in the middle of the table.

James considered how to address the subject of this person who was to come into the household. It was a delicate problem. Joseph would not like that his son had listened in on the talk of these visitors, but James very much wanted to understand the changes that lay ahead for the family—and for himself. He had to ask.

"Father," the boy ventured, "when will Mary come to our house?"

Joseph's eyebrows went up slightly, and his hand paused in delivering a morsel of lamb to his mouth. Then he smiled.

"You are always the curious one," he said. "You heard my talk with the men?"

"Yes, Father."

Joseph thought of scolding, though he didn't think of it

seriously. "No matter," he said. "You would have learned of these things soon enough. Have you told your brothers?"

"No, Father."

"Then please don't. I will tell them what is to happen."

"What *is* to happen, Father?"

When this morning's discussion on the porch had turned to specific details of Mary's coming, the voices of all three men grew softer, and James could not hear as much. He knew only that a marriage was to take place between his father and Joachim's daughter.

Joseph ate the piece of lamb, then said, "Mary will leave the temple before the turn of the new year. Then, a betrothal will be announced. A date for the wedding will be set at that time. There is no urgency, and I have projects that will take me way from Nazareth for several weeks. My journey has been planned for some time. We will marry after I return."

"Does Mary know?" the boy asked.

"Her father will speak with her," Joseph said. He reached to take some olives from the tray, then hesitated, aware once more of his lack of hunger, and clasped his hands together with his arms resting on the table.

James noticed. "You should eat, Father," he said.

Joseph looked at the boy fondly. "And so should you, my son."

"Then, we will eat together," James said.

Joseph smiled, and the two of them took food from the tray and ate. After a time, James, renewed his questioning.

"Do you think that Mary will want to marry you?"

"Mary is an obedient daughter," said Joseph. "And from what Joachim and Zacharias say, it seems that she is a bright girl. If this is so, then she will see that it is the best way for her to live in the manner she—Well, she will see the rightness of the arrangement her father has made for her. I am certain she will agree."

"Where will she sleep, Father?"

"The upper room. That will be her home. I will set it aside for her use only. Mary has known a life of prayer and study. And since she can no longer have that in the temple, then she will have it in her own home. Or at least something as near to it as possible."

"The upper room is where you and I sleep," said James.

Since his relationship with Mary would be of a different nature than that with his late wife, Escha, Joseph had naturally assumed the girl would require separate quarters. He would, in consequence, remove himself to the lower level of the house. But only now did it occur to him that dedicating the upper room to Mary's exclusive use would mean evicting his son from the space in which parent and child had shared their nights since James was small.

"Oh. Yes. I—I am sorry, my son. I must confess, I did not think about..."

The expression on James' face made Joseph realize what disruption this would bring to the well-established order and rhythms of his son's life. It was a point of pride to Joseph that he had always been a good father, able to provide a secure home and an orderly pattern of living for his sons and daughters. He observed how some families paid little heed to the conditions in which their children lived. He knew that far too many of the urchins glimpsed on the streets of Nazareth slept in the straw of animals— and looked it. Now, Joseph felt that, in helping Joachim, a man whom he respected, he had ignored the needs of his own flesh and blood.

"I truly am sorry, my son," he said.

James saw guilt in his father's eyes, and it stabbed him in his heart. "Where will *you* sleep, Father?" the boy asked.

"Here. In this room," said Joseph.

"Than I will sleep here with you," James said. "This will be *our* home."

If there was effort in the smile which James showed to his father, Joseph accepted it as a sign of love.

"Yes, my son," he said. "This will be our home. Of course, Mary will be welcome in it."

"Yes, Father. Mary will be welcome."

Escha had been right. James was the child of his old age. He loved the boy in a special way, and he resolved that whatever adjustments might have to be made, he would let nothing become an impediment to his relationship with this last and cherished son.

CHAPTER TWO
MEETING MARY

Many a man claims to have unfailing love,
but a faithful man who can find?
(Proverbs 20)

What an odd feeling it was for Mary to be in her father's house, even on a visit. During all the temple years, she had seen it only two times —once when she visited during an illness her mother had suffered, and again when Anna died. It was true that she had a vague recollection of running around the fountain in the center of the court as a tiny child, but that was little more than a sequence of half-formed and fleeting images. The thought of living in this place on a permanent basis gave her a feeling that was odd, indeed. But her life in the virgins' quarters would draw to a close in a matter of months, and the only possibility of returning would be in late age, after the monthly flow of blood would have ended and she no longer faced recurring impurity.

Was she sad at the turn her life would soon take? Mary could not say that, exactly. This was her ancestral home, and in any case, she had always known—it had been made amply clear to her, as to all the other girls—that temple life was of limited duration. Each virgin would eventually leave, to be succeeded by another in an ongoing cycle of prayer, study, and service to the Lord in his earthly dwelling. It was the will of Heaven that she should return to her father's house, and she had been told that this brief visit—two weeks, arranged by Zacharias—was preparation for that time soon to come.

If she was to live here, Mary could certainly console herself that the home of Joachim was a nice place to live. Hiram, the steward, had taken pains to see that her room would be comfortable. The chamber was considerably larger than the simple cell she occupied in the temple precincts. Two tall windows brought air and light. Big, down-filled pillows and coverlets were provided. A bronze, Roman-style brazier sat in the center of the floor for warding off the chill of night. Hiram stressed that the master's daughter had only to ask and her merest need would be met.

It was all more than Mary was used to. It made her feel small—even smaller than she was, which was quite petite. It also made her confused about what she should be doing. At this time of the evening she would normally have been preparing for bed after returning from prayer with the other virgins. But outside the rarefied world of the temple precincts, only men met to recite the evening service, women being exempt from such religious obligations because of their household duties. Mary didn't know what, if any, duties she would have in her father's household. She had no sense of what to expect or what was expected of her.

Perhaps it was too soon to concern herself with all of that. Her father would no doubt make his will clear to her —share with her how he saw her life with him—that is, when they had the chance to speak at length. Joachim had met Mary in the court upon her arrival from Jerusalem with Hiram and two other male servants who had brought her. Father and daughter shared an embrace and a few words of greeting, then he placed his hands on her head and offered a blessing of welcome.

But she had been tired after the journey and taken aback to see how shockingly frail he had become. The change from when she had seen him at the burial of her mother was pronounced. Joachim realized the effect his appearance had on his daughter. He insisted that she rest, and she was pleased to oblige. Her expectation was that they would dine together, so she was surprised when Hiram led a serving girl into her room later with food for Mary to take alone. Her father ate irregularly these days, the steward explained, but Joachim would speak with her that evening.

In correspondence with her father, Mary had obtained his assurance that she could retain her virginity when she left the temple precincts. Whatever the other circumstances of this new life to come, she would continue in her devotion to the Holy One of Israel. She would pray and she would study. If Heaven willed it, one day she would go back to Jerusalem.

Mary turned at the sound of soft footsteps in the doorway. It was Joachim.

"My daughter," he said, entering.

The girl rose. "Father."

"Are you rested, my dear child? I hope this room pleases you."

"I am rested, my father. And the room is fine. It is big."

Joachim smiled. There was a stool under one of the windows, and he sat, easing himself down with a difficulty which Mary could not help noting.

"Yes. No doubt it is different from the quarters to which you are accustomed," he said. "Forgive me for coming to you so late. I slept. These days, I sleep a great deal. As you can see—as it must be plain to you—my age is heavy upon me."

"What can I do to help you, my father?"

"Your being here helps me, child. It is a tonic to my tired old body. I rejoice in your youth and beauty. It refreshes."

Mary would have blushed at the compliment, but for the ache she felt watching the old man struggling as he was.

Joachim glanced up at the window behind him, then back at his daughter. "The cool of the night begins to come," he said. "My bones feel the chill so quickly now. That is a surprise of age. When you are young, coolness is pleasantly invigorating. In age, it attacks."

"Shall I light the brazier, Father?" Mary asked, eager to serve.

"No, no. I won't stay long. Your journey was hard. You must be to your bed, and I to mine." He laughed. "There, you see? I will sleep again. It seems that is all I do now."

Mary tried to smile in return. Joachim gestured toward the floor in front of him. She sat.

"My daughter," the old man said, "I realize that you have just arrived. And all that lies ahead of you—after your days in the temple come to an end—it will be new and unfamiliar. I would not be insulted if you feel a bit unsure, even frightened."

"This is your home, Father. And so it will be mine—as you and Mother always told me."

"Yes, it is your home." He was thoughtful for a moment. "What might your life have been like if you had grown up here? What joy might we have shared—you and your mother and me?" Another quiet moment. "Well...we shall never know. You belong to the King of the Universe, and it is right that you have served him."

"And soon I will serve *you*, Father."

Joachim smiled again. "That is a thought to warm my chilled bones," he said, and reached out to touch the side of Mary's small face with its delicate, sharply delineated features, the dark hair, those big eyes. "But, my child, surely you can see that I am a sick man. It was a joy to me when my late life was blessed by the Lord's gift of a daughter. Now it is a sadness that you come again when so little of my life is left to me." He peered deeply into those eyes. "But that too is the will of the Holy One, blessed be He."

Mary tried to speak, but could find no words to counter what was so plainly true.

Joachim had hoped for inspiration on how to begin what he expected to be a hard talk, but none was forthcoming. It would have been a blessing to have Mary with him, to enjoy her vitality for a few precious months. But she would soon return to Jerusalem, and each day's pain and travail added weight to the truth he knew all too well, that the end of his life was near. He could not be certain that he would last until the close of the year and the completion of her term in the temple. No delay was possible in broaching a difficult subject. Artfulness and tact were luxuries which time did not permit him. Mary would have to be presented with her destiny.

"What is essential now," Joachim continued, "is that you be taken care of when I am gone."

"Father, please do not speak of such—"

"My daughter...it is unfair that change should heap itself so quickly upon change in the life of one so young and innocent." His smile, as he looked upon the face of his beloved girl, was one of perfect fatherly love. "But these things must be said. I will die soon. That is a fact which cannot be avoided. And it is why the honored Zacharias made provision for you to come to me now, just months before you are scheduled to leave the temple."

"It *was* unexpected," said Mary.

"And highly irregular, I am sure. Zacharias understands that you will soon be orphaned."

"Father, surely I will see you at year's end."

"If the Lord allows."

"And after that—your home...*my* home..."

"There are relations, Daughter," Joachim said, "—distant relations that have legal claim on my properties. I cannot be sure whether my lands will continue to be held in one parcel or sold off. You will receive a bequest, of course, and it is substantial. I have structured things in a way that is a bit unconventional, but my plans will not be contested. The servants will also have their reward for years of dedication. All of this will be covered largely by the disposal of the house. It is of no small value. But that means it will belong to someone else."

Mary was suddenly distressed. "Then...where will I live?" Joachim held up his hand, and his face showed an expression with which he sought to be reassuring. "I have made an arrangement, my child. I'm convinced it is the best way for you to be protected and cared for. But the terms require that you consent to it willingly."

Mary was confused. Having just arrived in her father's house, and anticipating the end of her years in the temple, she was facing yet another change ahead. She realized that Joachim had the power to compel his daughter's acceptance of any arrangement he might have made. Indeed, he was under no compulsion to consider her feelings at all. But Mary sensed from her father's tone that she was being asked to make a choice of great significance to her entire life.

She raised herself to her knees. "What is this...arrangement, Father?"

Joachim looked at the small figure of his daughter who knelt before him, and he saw in her great strength. A memory of Mary as a three year-old, climbing the temple steps with a courage of which she was not even conscious flashed into his mind.

"I have spoken with Joseph, the carpenter and builder...just a little more than a week ago. He lives here in Nazareth, and he...has agreed to take you...as his wife."

Suddenly Mary felt her entire being flush with alarm. "But, Father," she said in near fright, "you promised that I could retain my virginity. You swore I could continue in my dedication—"

Both of Joachim's hands went up this time. "Yes, Daughter, yes," he said quickly. "This is my pledge to you, and I keep it. I promise."

"Then...I don't under—"

"Joseph is an older man. He is widowed with children, most of them grown. He is a man of great piety and virtue.

He has my complete trust. And...he promises that he will renounce all husbandly demands upon your person. You will live in your own quarters within the family compound. He will treat you as a daughter."

Mary searched her mind for any awareness of who this builder, Joseph, might be. But her life had been spent away from Nazareth, and there was no image or piece of local information to which she could attach a thought. She felt a spinning in her head. Married? She was to be married? Even under such terms as her father described—a husband who would claim no conjugal rights—this was too much for her to contemplate. In a very real sense, it was too much to be believed.

"I am confident that you will find great comfort and happiness in the house of Joseph," Joachim continued. "His sons and their families all live there. That is, three of the sons are married. With their wives and children they all live on the grounds. They each have their own quarters. And there is a younger son, as well. A fine boy, somewhat younger than yourself. He is a budding scholar."

Mary could hear her father's voice as he recounted the details of Joseph's home and family and the terms of his arrangement with this man who would be her husband. But it was as if he was talking from a distance.

"And of course," Joachim expounded further, "because his sons are there, you will remain in the family, even when Joseph has departed. The sons will care for you. They will have an obligation to you as their stepmother. So you will always be protected and have a home."

After some more minutes of elaboration, the old man recognized the dazed look on his daughter's face. He understood that the prospect of such an extreme shift in the direction of her life was perhaps more than she could take in all at once.

"But then," he said, "we can speak of this in the morning. It is much for you to think about, and you must rest."

"Yes, Father," she said vaguely. "I must rest."

Joachim gathered up his strength and pulled himself to his feet. "Please know, Daughter, that my greatest concern —my *only* concern—is for your well-being. I cannot go to my grave knowing that I haven't protected you, that I left you a prey to the teeth of those who might do you harm, as the psalm says. You are yet so, so young." He started to make his way slowly across the room to the doorway. "Please think of these things. We will speak more tomorrow."

She was still kneeling before the stool where Joachim had sat. He was out of the room when she finally collapsed back on her heels and said, in a quiet, distracted voice, "Yes, Father, we will speak more tomorrow."

Mary did not expect to sleep when she turned to her bed. For some time, her mind whirled with thoughts and wild conjecture about this new life her father had planned for her. But then, tiredness overcame her. Once asleep, she slumbered deeply the entire night, with dreams that were surprisingly pleasant. Light breaking through the two windows woke her gently, and she felt refreshed and calm. She prayed the morning service upon rising, interrupted by the serving girl who brought a basin of water. The servant realized that she had disturbed her mistress, and was embarrassed. But Mary's gentle smile set the girl, who was about her own age, at ease, and she withdrew. After Mary had finished her prayers and washed, she put on a clean white tunic and shawl, then went out to the court, where she found her father reclining on a divan. It was situated in the center of a small pergola with an overhead lattice from which wide swaths of cloth were suspended at their corners to provide shade. A low, round table sat beside him.

Joachim's face lit at her approach. "My daughter," he called. "Be seated. Food is coming. You slept well, I hope."

Mary deposited herself on a cushion. "Yes, Father. Very well."

"I am glad."

Joachim raised himself on one arm, which shook slightly under the effort. Mary reached toward him to help, but he waved her off. "My child, I have sent word to Joseph, asking that he come to us this evening. We will dine, and you will see for yourself what a fine and noble fellow he is. Though if you asked anyone in Nazareth, they would confirm his honorable character."

It was obvious Joachim intended to persist in the effort to convince his daughter of the rightness of what he was proposing. Mary did not feel so much put under pressure by her father's single-mindedness as she felt sad for him. If this was a matter of such urgency, he must surely feel the angel of death close at hand. She thought about Joachim's wistful question of the night before. What might their life have been like if she had not spent her childhood in the temple? But such musings profited nothing, and she did not let herself dwell on the thought.

"Yes, my father," she said. "I am happy to meet this

Joseph. I realize that you have my best interest at heart. And we shall see."

Joachim was encouraged by Mary's openness to his intention. The girl had always shown great wisdom— wisdom well beyond her years. It had been remarked upon in the temple.

Mary spent most of the day exploring her father's house and grounds. Hiram the steward set his young son, Mordechai, the task of leading the master's daughter on a tour. Mary lost herself in exploring barns, animal pens and the meadow where a small herd of cattle grazed. Mordechai took her to the top of a hill from which the whole of Nazareth could be viewed. She asked the boy if he might point out the house of Joseph the builder, but he was uncertain which it might be.

She did not converse with her father again during that day. The old man took to his bed once more, though not before urging Mary to rest herself when the sun would be highest in the sky. His urging reflected sincere fatherly concern, but he also wanted her to be fresh and at her best for the meeting with Joseph.

It was late afternoon, at the conclusion of her explorations, when Mary heeded his entreaty. She found a tray with fruit waiting for her in her room, but she ignored it and lay down on the bed. Not long after, she awoke, surprised to realize that she actually had drifted off to sleep. She sat for a time on the floor, praying. Anxiety had begun to take hold again, and she asked the King of the Universe to give her strength and clarity of mind for the decision ahead.

After praying, Mary went out to find the serving girl. She asked for water, that she might wash in preparation for the evening, and the girl quickly brought a basin. When she had finished cleansing herself, Mary dressed in the last of the three white tunics that were the main elements of her wardrobe from the temple. She would have to attend to laundry tomorrow, and she wondered if she would be permitted to wash her own clothes.

So far, all her needs had been met by the serving girl—whose name, it now occurred to Mary, she did not know. That would have to be rectified. The girl seemed shy and sweet. Perhaps she might be a friend. After all, Mary thought, was she, herself, not a servant in the temple? There were many chores along with prayer and study. Mary was well acquainted with the work of human hands.

It was Hiram who came to tell the master's daughter that her father desired her presence. Rising, she straightened her tunic, fastened her hair in back with a linen ribbon died dark blue, then took up a pale blue shawl, which was the mark of the temple virgins, and draped it over her head. She followed the steward down a corridor and into the common room. Joachim was seated on the divan, brought in from the pavilion where he had reclined at the morning meal. There was a man standing by, holding himself erect, a walking staff in his hand.

Nervous as she was, Mary willed herself to not let her feelings show, but she was unable to restrain her eyes from going to the visitor. He was tall and muscular, with the large hands one would expect of a man who worked in timber or stone. Mary might have described him as handsome, for someone his age, which she could see was sufficient for him to be her father—though not nearly as old as her actual father. There was still color in the man's hair and beard, a fine black among the strands of gray. She doubted he was as old as Joachim had been when she was born. Still, in no sense would he be called young. Perhaps her father was right and she *could* be confident of having her virginity respected.

Joachim noted the girl's entry into the room and extended a hand in her direction. "Ah, the treasure of my life, my daughter, Mary." Then, turning to his guest, the old man said, "And this, Daughter, is my esteemed friend, Joseph, son of Jacob, of the line of David."

Joseph bowed his head. "I am honored to meet the daughter of Joachim."

Mary lowered her eyes demurely and bowed her head in return. Joachim bade Joseph to place his staff down and set himself at ease on a chair made with curved wooden supports that crossed each other front and back in the Roman style, and a cushioned seat. He gestured for his daughter to join him on the divan. There was very little ease in any of them, since all understood the importance of this first meeting. A conversation then ensued with difficulty. They spoke of Mary's time in the temple, about which Joseph seemed genuinely curious. Then Joachim prodded Joseph into a long discourse about his family: his sons and their wives, his grandchildren, the life of his household, his business.

Joseph spoke of learning the carpenter's trade as a boy, of how his father had first assigned him the task of pulling nails from recovered timbers and broken implements, and straightening them for reuse. It was a lesson in frugality that had stayed with him through life—and also a lesson in carefulness. He would roll each nail on a stone, striking it on all sides until it was straight enough to be hammered into new wood without bending under a blow. He taught his own son, Josis, to do the same, and many were the fine Greek villas in Sepphoris whose headers and lintels were fastened by the proud and ancient nails of Nazareth. Mary laughed at the story, and Joseph seemed pleased to have amused her.

Most of the talk was between Joachim and Joseph, which was fine with Mary. Any self-possession gained living in the temple was not quite strong enough to overcome the natural shyness of a young girl in the presence of two older men. And anyway, she understood that too much womanly chatter was not held as becoming.

She quietly watched the interplay going on before her, sensing a confident nature in Joseph. And a warmth. He spoke about his family with great tenderness, which Mary found appealing. In her father she observed enthusiasm, an engagement in all this talk that seemed to lift him out of his decrepitude. She now fully understood that Joachim had much hope invested in this prospective match. This was his will for her. That much was clear.

Was it the will of Heaven? How could she know?

Servants brought in dinner, and the men continued to dominate the conversation as they ate. Mary continued to observe. When the meal was finished and they had said the blessing, she begged her father's leave to absent herself, and went to her chamber. It was her intention to sit for a few minutes to reflect and pray.

On entering the room, she saw that a vase of flowers had been placed on the small table near her bed. Lilies. They had always been a favorite. They grew in the temple precincts, and she had often collected them to decorate the virgins' quarters. Mary smiled when she saw the trumpet-shaped blooms, wondering if her father had directed that they be put there as a gentle encouragement to her positive evaluation of Joseph. Then she wasn't sure if he even knew about her love for lilies. There was no recollection of ever mentioning it.

Mary sat in prayer for a time, until she heard voices in one of the windows. She stood and peered out into the twilight. Joachim was walking in the court, haltingly, supported by the muscular arm of Joseph. The two men were still deep in their conversation. Watching them, she began to wonder at Joseph's willingness to participate in this arrangement for her care.

The talk at dinner had made it clear to Mary that he was in no need of any money Joachim might offer for her sustenance. And while widowed—for some years, apparently—he had his family, even a young son. James, Joseph had called him. These were all the comforts he should need to carry him to the end of life. And yet, he was willing to take a girl, young enough to be his daughter, into his home, and bind himself to a promise of chastity toward her.

Joachim was most certainly convinced of Joseph's integrity. And even after only this brief meeting, Mary did not question her father's judgment. There was something about this builder, this carpenter, that gave her—if not certainty—at least a kind of comfort, though she could not explain why. Comfort was something she dearly wished for at this moment. For, in truth, her situation offered no real alternative to marriage. Joachim was dying. Who would take her in?

But no. It was not resignation which Mary felt. She was experiencing something very different from just acceptance, from a mere facing of the inevitable. Suddenly, unexpectedly, she realized that she felt confident. Restored. Almost serene. It was the first time she had dared to feel any such way since realizing she was nearing the age when she must leave the temple.

Mary turned from the window, and her eyes fell on the lilies again. She went to the vase and snatched up the flowers, perhaps only in a small, unthinking effort to associate a tangible thing of earthly beauty and fond memory to the warmth which now radiated inside her. She left her chamber and went back to the common room, intending to wait for Joachim and Joseph to return. But then she spotted Joseph's walking staff where it lay behind the Roman-style chair.

The table had been cleared of the dinner remains, and on impulse, she set the flowers down on its surface. Then she went to get the staff off the floor and brought it to the table. Her hands reached to the back of her head, under the light blue shawl, and she untied the linen ribbon, setting her hair loose over her shoulders. Mary gathered up the flowers around the end of Joseph's staff, fastening them with the narrow, dark blue cloth strip. She propped the staff, with its new decoration, up against the chair for the men to find. They would understand its meaning.

Mary, the virgin daughter of Joachim, looked at this symbol she had created, crude and girlish as it was, and she grinned in satisfaction. Then she left the common room and returned to her bed chamber.

CHAPTER THREE

NEW PROSPECTS FOR JAMES

I have chosen him, that he may charge his children and his household after him to keep the way of the Lord by doing righteousness and justice.

(Genesis 18)

J oseph's sons were perplexed at the imminent coming of Mary, though not at all surprised. They knew their father to be a man of charity. Indeed, it was held in the family that if angels came to test the hearts of men, as the holy books recorded, then a goodly batch had passed through their gate, found the food pleasing, and sent back word to others in Heaven to come and sample the fare. What else could account for the long line of down-at-their-luck relatives and misbegotten wanderers who had taken refuge in the house of Joseph over the years?

To Josis, much the eldest, it was a matter of some humor that this mere slip of a girl would be their new stepmother. "That is the sort of match made in royal families," he said. "I guess the blood of David still marks us as special."

His brothers laughed. Joseph smiled, but then waved the levity to a close.

"My sons," he said, "it is important that you understand the delicate nature of this arrangement. Mary's situation is unusual, and not one which most people would understand or appreciate. Some might even find it shocking that a young girl would refuse to marry in the usual sense, forgo children, live in so solitary a manner. They might think her a shameless child, one who is rebellious toward her father, unconcerned for her family name, even peculiar in her desires. Ugly ideas quickly become wicked words, and Joachim is at great pains to shield his daughter from suspicion and gossip."

"But Father," said Simon, "surely people could respect the pious intentions of a girl raised in the temple."

"If only!" said Judas. "I know plenty who are not so filled with regard for the temple. And they have reasons. There are complaints enough about priests living well on the temple tax. No surprise if people harbor ill thoughts about a house full of women within the precincts."

Judas' observation was solidly based. Resentment toward the temple ran deep, not least because the high priest was chosen, installed and maintained by the king. Herod, that reviled, half-Jew vassal of the Romans, had inveigled his way onto the throne. He was chosen by Marcus Antonius, conqueror of Jerusalem, as the least worst of the options available to govern the troublesome Jewish homeland.

That the high priest should be under the thumb of such

a vile pretender as Herod was a festering sore on the body of Jewish religious life.

No matter that the king had expanded and beautified the temple to an extent that made it legendary throughout the world. Most people were suspicious of the priestly administration. The separatist sect known as the Essenes had abandoned temple sacrifice entirely.

Joseph knew that Judas, his quiet second son, was inclined toward reticence and the least likely to offer his thoughts. "If your brother perceives the possibility of suspicion and rumor," he said, "we should all expect it. Tongues may wag about the difference in age between Mary and myself." He shook his head in acceptance of the inevitable joking.

"So be it. But in all other respects, this marriage must appear ordinary.

The world need not—and it must not—know that there is anything unusual between the daughter of Joachim and myself."

"But...Father..." said Simon hesitantly. "If after awhile...there are no...children?"

"That can be ascribed to my age," Joseph answered firmly. "If the explanation does not suffice... Well, let people think what they will of me. My duty—the duty of all in this family—is to protect Mary's honor and privacy. I know I can count on your help in that."

His sons nodded in agreement.

Then Josis added, "Our wives must be made to understand. They will treat Mary with the utmost warmth and consideration, I'm sure. But there will have to be explanations prepared for the children. And it would be most helpful if all our stories were consistent. What can be said about this new—" He paused, smiling again, "—grandmother?"

The others laughed.

"Not quite grandmother, I think," Joseph said, sharing in his sons' amusement. "Mary will do. Just Mary. The older children can be counseled against taking too close an interest in their grandfather's home life. And over time, the younger ones will come to understand how the pieces of a family fit together, no matter how complicated it all may seem."

Joseph turned to his youngest son who was seated to the side of his elder brothers. "James will set the example," he said, tipping his head in the boy's direction. "He understands the nature of this arrangement. His acceptance of Mary and his ease in the household will show that all is as it should be. The children will observe that and follow his lead."

"Yes, our scholar will handle things," said Josis, and stretched his arm over to the boy, knocking off his cap and tousling his hair playfully.

James picked the cap off the floor and, with a smirk, swatted it in the direction of his eldest brother. Everyone shared in the lightness of the moment. What the others could not see behind the horseplay was a deep division in the boy's feelings. James understood the trust which Joseph was placing in him, and he took it as a sign of his father's great love. At the same time, it was fearful to think that his family's high regard among the people of Nazareth might, to a considerable measure, be dependent upon him. His job was to influence the children in their acceptance of this new family member. Children observe, but children talk.

"In any event," Joseph said, "there is time. Mary

departs for Jerusalem after Sabbath, and then there are yet many weeks until she completes her term and returns to Nazareth. But speak with your wives. If they have questions, have them come to me. I will explain further."

The brothers knew that Joseph had their wives' trust. Not one of the three women would hesitate to approach him with any concern—a situation not at all common. How many Nazareth wives would be so at ease with the family head? Many the wife who did all she could to avoid the imperious gaze of her husband's father—or worse, his mother. And so it was with surprise that each brother later encountered a reaction that was something a bit less than joy over the news of the family's expected new member.

Sarah, Judas' wife, found it very strange that any woman should wish to avoid having children. "Is it not odd," she asked her husband, "that this girl should dedicate herself to the Creator and yet turn from His command to be fruitful? What sort of piety is that? She has studied the holy books like a boy—does this make her despise her womanhood?"

Salome, the wife of Josis, thought it was highly unfair of Joachim to have bound Joseph to such an obligation. "Your father deserves the comfort of a true wife in his old age, not the cares of raising a daughter he will never be able to give to another man," she said.

The strongest objection came from Simon's wife, Zipporah, youngest of the women. With three small children in her house, two not yet trained from soiling themselves, she saw this girl as an extra weight to be borne by the wives. "What does this mean for us?" she complained.

"We all have our own to tend. Are we to serve this little princess from the temple who plans on having no babies?"

Next morning, the three brothers commiserated over their wives' reactions. And during the following days, Joseph too became aware that his beneficence toward an old and dying friend was not being received well within his own walls. He smoothed what feathers he could by taking each daughter-in-law aside to assure her that Mary was quite capable of caring for herself and might even prove a great help.

Joseph also brought his two daughters, Lydia and Assia, into his confidence, and found them to be only marginally more receptive to the news than their brothers' wives had been. Lydia closely echoed Salome's concern about Joseph taking on this added responsibility. And while her sister professed that she was proud of their father's generous spirit, she too was worried that his act of kindness might lead to heartache. In the end, Joseph decided that he must entrust the peace of his family to the King of the Universe and the passage of time.

The weeks after Mary's return to the temple passed in the daily activities of life. There was a steady stream of orders for the finely crafted wooden furniture, tools and implements made by Josis, who had taken over the Nazareth shop. The eldest son had learned much since his boyhood introduction to the craft as his father's nail straightener. Josis had become a true master of the woodworker's art, Joseph conceding that his son's manual skills now surpassed his own.

Judas and Simon alternated days tending their flock grazing in the pasture rented from Joachim and nurturing the olive grove they were trying to establish beyond the east wall of the family compound. The wives saw to their daily routines of household chores and children. And James pursued his studies.

For Joseph himself there were the crews to supervise in Sepphoris and much consultation with clients over endless construction details and plan modifications. This was frequently done in the company of his able assistant, Lucillus, a gentile God-fearer whom most people referred to as Lucillus the Greek. That appellation was inaccurate. Lucillus was a son of Carthage, born a slave. But the name stood as a brief summation of a varied and accomplished life.

Quick-witted as a boy, Lucillus had learned to read and cipher by listening in on the lessons of the Roman child he had been assigned to serve on the island of Cyprus. He caught the eye of the child's father, a trader and owner of ships who took him from his youthful charge and set him a variety of tasks. As he grew into a sturdy lad with the black hair and dusky skin of his ancient race, Lucillus acquired greater trust and responsibility for his master's affairs.

The master eventually relocated his household and business to Palestine, setting up in a substantial villa in Caesarea. So fond had he become of his trusted servant that he granted Lucillus his manumission.

When the master died, the son of the family, whom Lucillus had served as a child, assumed leadership of the firm. He proved much less a businessman than his father had been. The company foundered, leaving Lucillus with his freedom but no work.

The wanderings that followed brought Lucillus to Sepphoris, where he met Joseph, who recognized the gifts that had been apparent to the old trader. Lucillus became Joseph's right hand, keeping the books, managing the store of supplies, helping to estimate the costs of projects, and paying the crews. Another of Lucillus' duties—though an unofficial one—was tutoring James in Greek and Latin. He also shared with the boy the considerable stock of tales, poems, songs and philosophical sayings picked up on the many errands he had run for his late master along the imperial trade routes.

It was Lucillus who, some weeks after Joseph's meeting with Mary, accepted a letter carried by a messenger from Ein Kerem, the Judean town where Zacharias resided. He took the missive to Joseph, who was seated with James at the midday meal.

"Forgive this intrusion," said Lucillus, holding out the small scroll. "A message from the honored priest, Zacharias."

Joseph broke open the seals and handed the scroll back to Lucillus, asking him to read it aloud. The message began with customary greetings, followed by a request to be forgiven for the delay in writing after their meeting with Joachim. Zacharias had been overcome by a strange event, he noted, one that shook him deeply and robbed him of his voice. This, Joseph took as a reference to some kind of illness. Then Lucillus read that Zacharias reported a great and unexpected blessing that had come upon his house. Elizabeth, his wife, had conceived.

"Remarkable," Joseph said. "The wife of Zacharias is of advanced age. And she will have a child? Blessed be the

Holy One of Israel. Zacharias and Elizabeth have always been without children. This is most remarkable, indeed."

Almost in passing, the priest expressed his joy at hearing that a contract for the marriage had been drawn between Joseph and Joachim.

And then the message turned to Joseph's youngest son. Zacharias cited his comment about James coming to Jerusalem to study, and he repeated the offer to arrange for a teacher. "When James has attained his maturity," Zacharias wrote, "send him to me, and as I promised, I will find him a place in the school of a learned scribe."

James, his mouth falling open, stared at his father. "Can this be true?" he asked.

Lucillus looked up from the scroll. "Zacharias is a holy man," he said, "a man of honor."

"And of much gratitude, it would appear," said Joseph thoughtfully.

He glanced at his son. "We must plan a great celebration for the day when you read in the synagogue. If you are going to study in Jerusalem, then celebrating will be in order. Not very many Nazareth boys have sat with the doctors of the Law."

"This will be a special thrill for Ezra, your teacher," said Lucillus.

"And for his Greek tutor?" said Joseph.

Lucillus smiled. "Quite special," he said.

"Then you shall be in charge of planning the big event," said Joseph.

"It will be my honor," said Lucillus, bowing broadly and sweeping one arm in front of him.

"Will it be like one of those grand Roman feasts you

observed in your world travels?" Joseph asked teasingly, an eye on James.

"Perhaps not so grand as that," his assistant said. "Our scholar mustn't be led astray by pagan delights. We shall celebrate in a way befitting the dignity of the occasion."

James, not really aware that he was the being made the object of their humorous banter, asked, "May I invite the other boys in the school—and the Rabbi Ezra?"

"Of course," Joseph said, "all the boys and the Rabbi Ezra. And the Sanhedrin and a deputation from the court of Herod. It will be an important day for the town of Nazareth and all of Galilee."

"Perhaps the king himself will attend," said Lucillus, "and the Augustus as well. I have contacts in Rome."

Now James caught onto the joke. "But my friends can come," he asked, "and the rabbi?"

"It wouldn't be a celebration without them," his father said reassuringly. "Lucillus will handle the preparations. But you must continue to work hard at your lessons. There are many more months ahead before this feast. And if the honored Zacharias is willing to recommend you for study in Jerusalem, you must be prepared to do him credit when the time comes."

"I will, Father, I promise," said James.

The rest of the letter was an expression of Zacharias' satisfaction that Mary had consented to the arrangement made on her behalf, followed by an ardent appeal for the blessings of Heaven upon Joseph and his entire family. To that end, Zacharias promised to make an offering of thanks in the temple.

"Mary is an exceptional young woman," the priest concluded. "All who have known her in Jerusalem speak with the highest regard for her piety and virtue. I am sure she will enrich your household, and that you will never have cause to regret this great deed you are doing."

As Lucillus read the letter's formulary closing with its elaborate expressions of hope for good health and well being, Joseph pondered the reservations expressed by his daughters and his sons' wives. He experienced a momentary and disturbing thought that women can be surprisingly clear of sight. But then he pushed the notion from his mind.

CHAPTER FOUR

THE HOUSEHOLD TOUCHED

*The angel Gabriel was sent from God to a city of Galilee called
Nazareth, to a virgin betrothed to a man whose name was Joseph.*
(Luke 1)

Aloud pounding on the gate set the dogs to
barking, and soon people stirred all throughout
the compound. A baby began to cry. Simon,
whose house was closest to the front, emerged into the
court with a woolen blanket wrapped around himself
from the shoulders. He opened a small port in the
wooden gate and looked through to the midnight visitor
outside.

"It is I, Hiram, steward of the house of Joachim," the
man on the other side said excitedly. "Please forgive this late
disturbance. I must see Joseph the carpenter. My master is
gravely ill—I believe he is dying—and he begs that Joseph
come to him with all speed."

Simon opened the gate and led Hiram across the court
and under the portico to the foot of the stairway that led to

the upper room where Joseph and James slept. "Father," he called up.

After a time, the bleary-eyed visage of Joseph appeared in the wooden enclosure at the top of the stairs.

"A thousand pardons, honorable sir," Hiram said. "My master, Joachim, begs your presence—and quickly, please, if you would be so kind. The end is near, and he needs to speak with you."

"A moment," said Joseph, disappearing back into the darkened room.

It had been several months since the dinner with Joachim and Mary, so Joseph wasn't surprised that the end was at hand. Since their marriage arrangement had been solidified, Joseph had prayed that his old friend might survive long enough to see his daughter return from the temple. The King of the Universe had blessedly granted that gift. But now the entire town was abuzz with Joachim's steep decline and imminent death.

"What is it, Father?" James asked with sleep in his voice. Joseph took a heavy cloak from a line of hooks by the door, pulled it over his hastily arranged tunic to shield himself from the night air, then placed a knitted cap on his head. "Joachim is dying," he said to the boy. "I must go to him. Go back to sleep, my son." He stepped into his sandals, tied them, and started for the door, then stopped, looking back at the boy. "Pray for my old friend."

"Yes, Father, I will."

Joseph descended the stairway and followed the steward through the court and out the gate. Simon secured it behind them, then went to calm the dogs and inform the others, who had arisen at the noise, of what was happening. Joseph and Hiram made their way through the town to the imposing home of Joachim, located at the end of the market street. Hiram's son, Mordechai, admitted them, and the two men went directly to the master's bedchamber.

Hiram's wife, the servants, all the members of the household were present in the room, which was dimly lit by oil lamps and the red glow of coals in a brazier. Mary sat on the floor beside the fragile and sunken form of her father. She bowed her head silently to acknowledge Joseph's arrival. Then she touched Joachim on the arm and spoke gently.

"My father—Joseph is here. He has come, as you asked."

The old man stirred, looked up searchingly, and through dim eyes recognized his visitor. He spoke weakly. "Joseph, my son."

"I have come, honored friend," Joseph said, feeling a reaction within his viscera at how little there was left of the man lying so slight before him.

Joachim lifted a hand, just a few inches, but enough to gesture Joseph to his bedside. Joseph knelt on the floor next to Mary.

"The Holy One is calling me now," he said in a voice thin and weak.

Joseph could barely hear, but he answered, "Blessed be He."

"It is time to act on the contract."

"I understand."

"Mary should go to your home now."

"I have prepared her a home of her own," said Joseph, "within our compound. I will take her when you have gone into the arms of the Lord."

Joseph looked at the girl, and she returned his glance to

reconfirm her assent to the agreement. Then Mary turned to the man who had brought Joseph.

"Hiram," she said, softly but with a firmness and authority one wouldn't have expected in a young girl.

The steward signaled all the others to leave.

"Good. Good." Joachim heaved a labored breath, long and with a rattling sound. "You will care for my...beautiful treasure."

"Yes."

"Announce the betrothal."

"I will, Joachim."

"No one will fail to understand...that my passing..." He paused, expended the effort of another difficult breath, and then continued. "There will be...no questions."

"Of course."

"The marriage can be held...at an appropriate time. Arrange everything as it should be. Then no one will ever ask... And Mary... She will be free to live according...to the terms of the contract. There...will be no questions."

"No questions, my dear friend."

Joachim struggled to extend his hand toward Joseph, who took it between his own.

"Thank you, Joseph. The King of the Universe...will bless you greatly."

Joseph tried to speak, but felt a catch in his throat.

Then with supreme effort, the old man turned his face toward Mary.

Joseph released his hand as Joachim tried to reach for the daughter he had possessed for so little time.

"Kiss your father, my child," he said weakly.

She leaned over and her lips brushed his forehead.

Joachim's eyes closed. "I go now," he said, then labored

for a final breath. "Hear, O Israel...the Lord our God...the Lord...is...one..." And the thin voice trailed off into a quiet wheeze. Then silence.

Joseph looked at Mary, and he saw tears running from her eyes for the father she had never really known.

The Rabbi Ezra was sent for and, with Joseph and Hiram, rites were arranged for Joachim, of blessed memory. Joseph's presence, both at the burial and during the days of receiving, was much noted by the townspeople. It had not been known that there was a close relationship between the carpenter and the great landowner. In fact, the only apparent connection was the rental of Joachim's pasture by Joseph's sons, Judas and Simon.

And yet it was Joseph who led the prayers of mourning and was at Mary's side most of the time throughout the seven days. This occasioned some curious whispering, which grew into a cycle of speculation, which soon became a whirl of conflicting rumors. The rumors gained velocity when, at the end of the sitting, Mary moved out of her family home and took residence in Joseph's house. But conjecture was put to rest the following Sabbath, when it was announced in the synagogue that Joseph and Mary were to be married. Surely a girl so recently returned from the temple, with no other family in town, would need to be cared for. It was a natural thing for her to be taken within the walls of her future husband.

As Joseph had predicted, local sympathy was leavened by much jovial banter about the groom-to-be of mature years and his promised bride of such tender and beguiling youth. But the joking was spiked by occasional, more pointed, speculation as to how much of Joachim's vast holdings the fortunate carpenter stood to have come his way in the bargain. Some of this reached the ears of Lucillus, who reported it to Joseph, who waved it away.

"Vain fancies," he said with a shake of the head. "Everyone is curious about other people's affairs. Imagination knows no bounds."

Daughter of a rich man though she was, Mary had little in the way of personal possessions. The extent of her worldly goods was the few clothes she had brought with her from the temple. Not wanting to see the daughter of Joachim come to her new husband empty-handed Hiram ordered that furnishings be carried from the chamber which had been provided for her in her father's house. These were installed in Joseph's upper room, recently cleared of his and James' belongings now moved downstairs.

Hiram brought some other furniture, as well, mementos of Mary's family home, which he thought it appropriate for her to keep. These included the divan, the Roman-style chair, and several other pieces. As space was limited in the lower room of Joseph's house, some of the items were placed under the portico and some stored in a shed next to Josis' workshop.

Hiram's last importation was the young serving girl, whom Mary had learned was named Hagar. Joseph hadn't considered that his bride would come with a servant, but on reflection he thought it shouldn't have been unexpected.

Mary, who still had not accustomed herself to being waited upon, expressed her discomfort to Joseph. "Hiram insists that I should have a girl to attend me," she told her future husband. "But in Jerusalem I attended to myself, and it has felt strange having someone fussing about. Still, Hagar is a pleasant, dutiful girl, and Hiram explained she is an orphan with no place else to go, now that my father's household is being dispersed. What is your will in this, Joseph?"

Though unanticipated, the only problem this situation seemed to pose was the question of where the girl would sleep.

Mary shrugged. "Hagar can sleep in my room."

"Well...until we can provide someplace for her," Joseph said.

"What shall I have her do?" Mary asked.

"Right now she can help you get settled," Joseph said. "After that... I'm sure there are ways for her to be useful. No doubt the family can think of many tasks. They will be pleased to have another set of hands."

Joseph was surprised to find that, when word of Hagar had spread throughout the household, his daughters-in-law were not pleased, but rather quite annoyed. The fact of a servant only compounded their reservations about Mary.

Once more it was Zipporah, wife of Simon, who made the harshest comment. "The princess has her own serving girl," she complained to her husband. "We shall see how helpful this Hagar is to the family when Mary wishes her linen aired or her bath drawn."

The brothers again found themselves commiserating over their wives' resentments, and again Joseph sought out each daughter-in-law. After encountering womanly skepticism at each of his three conversations, all he could do was pray that serenity might reign over his home.

It didn't. Joseph's attempts to introduce Mary into the

daily life of the family met with an atmosphere of icy discontent. It soon became apparent that Hagar was an impediment to Mary's acceptance, which was Joseph's primary concern. He shared this conclusion with Mary, who urged him to give it more time.

"I don't think that Hagar is the problem," she said. "Maybe they just don't trust me because I was in the temple. People don't understand temple girls. They think we place ourselves above everyone else. But I will try to help them like me. I will show them that I don't put on airs."

"That may not be easy with your own serving girl here," said Joseph, whose unhappiness over the attitude of his sons' wives was clear to Mary.

In the end, she agreed it probably would be best if Joseph could find a different situation for Hagar. Two days later, the house of the Rabbi Ezra included a servant, on a stipend provided by Joseph the builder. This helped to assuage feelings, at least partially. Other seeds of good will were sown when Mary took it upon herself to approach the wives, offering them their choice of Joachim's furniture.

"These pieces are very nice, but I have no use for them," she said.

"And since I lived so long away from home, they stir no memories of my parents. Please—if you would care to have anything that is here, take what you wish. Consider it a blessing from my dear father."

While there remained a noticeable chill, Mary's gesture was a small further step toward relieving it, and Joseph dared to hope for better times ahead. It occurred to him that he had glimpsed in this young girl the gift of wisdom.

That was all to the good, because after Mary's third

week in the compound, Joseph announced that he and Lucillus had to make a trip.

A shipment of wood beams for one of the Sepphoris projects was to be received at the port of Caesarea. These pieces had been cut and shaped in Lebanon according to rigorous specifications. They would have to be inspected, and overland transport arranged. The entire process would likely be concluded in less than a month, depending on the arrival time of the ship. This was always variable, and someone had to be on hand at the port throughout the entire span of time during which the ship might arrive, since unattended cargo was likely to disappear.

A date for the wedding could be set and made public upon Joseph's return.

Mary had taken over the care of Joseph's living quarters, and also tried to make herself available to the wives whenever they needed help with various household tasks. But the daily schedule of her prayers, which she maintained scrupulously, continued to set her apart from the other women. It seemed to them a very odd thing indeed for a girl to pray the services. There even was some shared anxiety among them that Mary might take it into her mind to pray with their husbands, which would be shockingly inappropriate. But who knew what presumptions might fill the head of a temple girl?

Salome expressed this concern to her father-in-law, who insisted such an idea was unthinkable. But admitting to himself that he couldn't really be sure what a girl of Mary's experience thought about such things, he queried Mary about her devotional practices—in as casual a manner as possible. She smiled knowingly, and assured him that her prayer life was entirely private. Joseph felt foolish for raising the question and more than a little annoyed at Salome for having prompted him to do so.

The only actual shortcoming that anyone could detect in Mary was a marked deficiency in cooking skills. She'd had kitchen duties in the women's residence, but only the most menial chores. She had never prepared a complete meal in her life. Consequently, she ate the food brought to Joseph's table by his daughters-in-law, which became another source or irritation among the women.

What the wives didn't realize was that Mary very much admired their ability to transform the fruits of the earth and the flesh of animals into appealing dishes for their families. But she recognized that each took great pride in her craft and guarded her own methods closely.

Since their suspicions of her were already so firmly set, Mary hesitated in asking them for instruction. That left her dependent on their diligence, even as it seemed to confirm their assumption that she took them for granted.

So it was with a certain amount of apprehension over the simmering unease in his household that Joseph prepared for his journey to Caesarea. While Lucillus waited in the court, making adjustments to the straps that held their packs fastened to the sides of a donkey, Joseph gestured to his son, James, and took the boy aside.

"Be attentive to Mary," he said. "Don't intrude, but keep aware, and see that she is well. I am worried for her happiness here. I realize now that it will take time for all to be comfortable with this."

"I will watch, Father."

"I pray that things will be improved when I return."

"And I, Father."

"If there is a problem, speak with Josis. He is the eldest."

"Yes, I will do that. May the King of the Universe watch over you, Father."

Joseph embraced the boy, then departed with Lucillus.

———

Mary and James took their meals in Judas' house on the first day that Joseph was gone, and in Simon's on the second. Mary expressed her appreciation to both Sarah and Zipporah, offering compliments, which were accepted with restrained grace. On the third day, Mary lingered after the midday meal in Josis' house. When Josis and James had departed, she screwed up her courage and asked Salome if she might be kind enough to teach her a few things about cooking.

"I trust that Joseph hasn't told you he is dissatisfied with the meals he's been getting," Salome said with a sideward look. Mary wasn't quite sure if the remark had been intended as a joke, and she was quick to reply nervously, "No, no—to the contrary. You are all such excellent cooks. Joseph seems delighted with the food, and I am also. And James, I'm sure. It is just that... Well, I have never learned to cook, and I feel I should know how...so that I can...do my part."

Salome could see the earnestness in the girl's face, and was struck by the thought that this was, after all, a mere child. Perhaps the women may have been too quick to judge Mary.

"Come back later and help me prepare the evening meal," she said, turning away.

Mary smiled, relieved, and offered a silent prayer of thanks to the Holy One.

Josis was surprised when, that evening at table, Salome mentioned how helpful his father's intended bride had been in preparing the meal.

"Oh?" He looked at the girl, whose eyes were turned down shyly. Then he looked at his wife, whose glance was also diverted. Then he looked at James, who, equally taken aback, returned his brother's surprised expression.

"That is...very good," said Josis.

Mary seemed to James especially cheerful when, later, he heard her up in her room praying the evening service. Her voice was louder than usual, with a lilting quality he'd not realized it possessed. Normally, what reached to the lower level was no more than a murmur, barely audible and certainly not sufficient to distract him from his own prayers, as her voice did tonight.

Unsettling as her sudden injection into the family had been, in the past three weeks James had observed Mary enough to decide that he did, in fact, like her. He felt bad at her obvious uneasiness, and he had prayed that his brother's wives could accept her. Salome's remark was a sign that perhaps things were turning in the right direction. He knew that, if it continued, his father would be pleased.

After completing his prayers, James went outside under the portico and sat on one of the stools, gazing across the court into the clear and star-filled sky. He and Joseph often took the evening air together for awhile before turning in to bed. It was a time to be alone with his father, a time he cherished. Joseph would ask about the day's lessons with the Rabbi Ezra and tell stories of the family and his own childhood in Bethlehem. James was especially fond of Joseph's recollections of Escha.

Hearing about his mother always made for crossed feelings in the boy. He was captivated when his father would reflect on how beautiful and vibrant Escha was and how she so loved her children. It would make him feel, oddly, both warm and sad at the same time. And the sadder he felt for this woman he could not recall, whose appearance he did not know, the more he wished to hear of her.

He thought about that now, looking at the stars, and it occurred to him that Mary's situation was not entirely dissimilar to his own. Her mother had not died when she was an infant, as his did, but Mary had grown up separated from her parents. Was that why she had chosen a life without children? It seemed to James that such an experience would push her in the opposite way, making her want a family all the more. But no. Apparently not. It was strange. Perhaps he would speak with her about it one day —when he knew her better.

James became aware that the court was exceptionally bright. He stood up and walked to the corner of the house at the end of the portico where he could look up into the southern sky. There was a brilliant full moon, a desert moon, a moon for which caravaners pray to illumine the night and protect them from the stealthy approach of thieves.

It seemed much brighter than usual, and especially large, the kind of moon that riveted one's gaze and was said to carry the mind away into strange musings.

The boy watched it for some time, examining the markings on its surface, which some called the face of the man. Then he realized he was tired and the hour was late. He walked around the side of the house to a screened area under the stairs that sheltered the privy. Then he went back inside the house and made his way across the room to a small oil lamp hanging over the table, and blew it out. He found his mat at the rear, lay down, and drew a blanket over himself. Sleep came in minutes.

James didn't know how long he'd slumbered. The chamber was still pitch dark, penetrated only by the indirect glow of moonlight in the small window. But something had broken his rest, some sound he could not name. Was it a human voice? Was it an animal outside?

He sat up on his mat, listening. There it was again. A voice. A wailing voice, though not loud. Were there words? He couldn't tell. But the voice was filled with feeling. Now frightened. Now happy. Frightened again. It was coming from above, he realized. Upstairs, from Mary's room.

James tossed his blanket aside, stood up, and groped his way across the dark space to the door and then outside to the foot of the stairs. He stood silently, straining to hear. Yes, it was Mary's voice. More of the strange, indecipherable utterances, then strained and rapid breathing, as if she had been sobbing, or perhaps laughing uncontrolled. Yet, James had not heard her cry or laugh. Was she in the grip of some frightening dream?

"Mary!" he called.

No response, just more of the inexplicable sounds.

James would never presume to invade Mary's privacy. His father had made it clear that she was to be left undisturbed when alone upstairs. But the boy had promised to look after her, and these strange sounds were cause for alarm.

He made his way softly up the steps to the doorway, open but shielded partly by a curtain. He could see her sitting on the floor, her face turned upward and transfixed by a shaft of light from one of the two windows in the upper room. Her slim body was trembling, as if in the kind of fit he had once seen a man fall into on the street outside the synagogue. Now her voice emitted a quiet series of oddly shifting sounds, almost like the words from some unknown language. Yet, for all of this, the features of her face were still, formed into a joyous smile, her lips barely moving, eyes wide.

"Mary," he said. "Mary, are you dreaming? Are you alright?"

She sat in this rapt state for some seconds, unaware of his presence in the doorway. Then she seemed to awaken, and turned her head to look at him, speaking at last. "Yes...I am...alright."

James waited, watching, his gaze drawn to her face, locked on her eyes, which were made bright, almost iridescent, by the moonlight.

Mary said nothing else, but rather sat quietly, the trembling and the odd sounds gone now.

After a time, the boy forced himself to turn away and started back down. He paused on the stair, glancing back, not understanding what he had seen, and feeling a disquiet that was like nothing he had ever experienced.

"Sleep well...Mary," he said.

CHAPTER FIVE

SHOCK AND DEPARTURE

During those days Mary set out and traveled to the hill country
in haste to a town of Judah.
(Luke 1)

Mary was unseen the next morning. She remained in the upper room when James went to Simon's house to break his fast, and did not emerge until after her midday prayers, when she went again to Salome to offer assistance with the cooking in hope of further instruction. Salome set her to work grinding barley with a small stone wheel, showing her how the corns were to be milled in order to produce a flour fine enough to be baked into bread.

It was tricky work, requiring coordination between feet and hands to keep the wheel turning steadily and an uninterrupted conveyance of corns under the grinding face and thence into powder. But Salome figured if the girl truly wished to learn how food was prepared, this most basic of tasks was a good starting point.

Throughout the afternoon Mary toiled at the barley, Salome stealing an occasional peek at her as she worked. The older woman was taken by the look on Mary's face: concentration punctuated by an inexplicable smile. Perhaps she was lost in thoughts of her days at Jerusalem.

Or maybe she was passing the time in continuous prayer. Or maybe anything—who could know the mind of a temple girl? Still, Mary obviously did not shy from the ordinary chores of life.

Salome began to think that perhaps Joseph was right and Mary would prove an asset to the family. After the sack of barley corns had been emptied, she inspected the girl's work and approved the fineness of the grinding, noting only a few fragments incompletely milled. She cut Mary's apology short. "Some always get through," Salome said. "These will be sifted out." And then she had the girl slice vegetables for a soup.

When James returned from the house of the Rabbi Ezra, he spotted Mary seated on a bench in the court outside Josis' front door. She was cutting onions on a board set in her lap, eyes focused intently on the work but slightly moist. He started to speak, but then held back, noting the smile on her face despite tears from the strong, irritating scent.

It was the same unearthly smile he had seen in the night. He stood for a moment, observing the girl's total concentration, and then was swarmed by a group of small nieces and nephews who were always happy when he came home from lessons.

In such a way did calm return to the house of Joseph.

Each day, after devotions, Mary went to Salome for cooking lessons, and also offered herself for chores to Sarah and Zipporah. Each day James went to the Rabbi Ezra. Life proceeded normally, with Joseph's absence most directly affecting Josis, whose carpentry orders were becoming backed up as he provided what oversight he could to the building projects. Several times he went to Sepphoris, where he had to make decisions on behalf of his father and attend to Lucillus' duty of paying the laborers.

James accompanied him on one of those trips, running errands for his brother while Josis visited the worksites. Going to the city was a treat for which the boy was always eager. He found the noise and bustle of city life a fascination, and listening to street chatter let him exercise the Greek and Latin acquired from Lucillus. That was challenging, since there were so many different kinds of people from so many places throughout the empire and they all spoke in such distinctive ways.

Legionaries, especially—some passing through Sepphoris from as far away as Gaul—pronounced their Latin words and phrases in accents tinged by strange languages which James could hardly imagine. They frequently departed completely from the legion argot in favor of their unknown native tongues. James strained to catch it all. But there was something else that—perhaps because he was getting older—drew his attention on this trip, a side of city life that was less fascinating than disturbing. It was how people behaved when they came into contact with other groups. Greeks, of whatever nationality, tended to behave toward Jews in a most superior way, their facial expressions and their ways of speaking laden with condescension, even outright mockery. The boy overheard derisive words and observed rude gestures, even catching an unpleasant glance directed at himself.

Jews, for their part, maintained blank faces in the presence of Roman soldiers or even the ordinary Greeks of the city. But out of sight and earshot, they expressed feelings of resentment and disgust. They would make rude gestures of their own or speak in vulgarities. James saw one man spit on the street after passing a pair of Greek women.

He shared these observations with Josis, who acknowledged that this was the way of life in places where the nationalities rubbed up against each other. It seemed to be especially so in the cities, like Sepphoris, where Greeks dominated.

"Father tells our men never to express themselves in such ways," Josis said, "even when no one is around. He insists the workers avoid our clients and all other Greeks as much as possible. He says we are here to work, not give vent to anger."

"Do the men obey?" James asked.

"They respect Father," Josis said. "And they like their pay."

Aside from that one excursion, most days followed the normal pattern of studies and household activity. Those weeks without Joseph passed undisturbed by any noteworthy incident. Except at night. Mary had taken to singing in her room, softly enough that it was unnoticed by anyone but James immediately below.

At first it caused him some concern. Mary's voice, though a bit muffled, was a sweet presence as he laid on his mat in the dark, and he worried that it might be wrong to listen, since the sound of a woman singing could be considered immodest. But some of the songs brought back memories of his sisters singing to him as a small child. He reasoned—perhaps with a bit of self-serving—that since he had not yet attained his maturity, and since Mary was soon to be his stepmother, and since all of her songs gave praise to the King of the Universe, then listening might not be sinful. So he allowed himself to enjoy the sound.

While she sang mostly in a lilting and sprightly way, sometimes Mary's voice took on an eerily somber quality. James wondered if there was some deep sadness hidden beneath the good nature she showed the family. Or perhaps it was fear revealing itself occasionally in these nightly recitals. But then, wouldn't such feelings rise within her, so recently uprooted from the temple, bereft of her only parent, and set down in the middle of a new home? On such nights, the desire for Joseph's return exceeded the boy's normal longing for him. James truly wished that Mary might receive some solace, but he didn't know what to do for her.

Anticipation of his father's wise counsel was unrewarded, however.

Nearly a month after Joseph's departure, Lucillus appeared at the gate of the compound. He informed the family that Joseph was detained at Caesarea. The ship bearing the consignment of carved beams had been delayed in its departure from Lebanon. Joseph had taken temporary employment with a local carpenter to stave off boredom while he was waiting, and Lucillus would assume direction of the Sepphoris projects until the master's return.

Josis felt a sense of relief, as he could now catch up on the pieces languishing unfinished in his workshop. James was disappointed, but he noticed that Mary suddenly looked strangely worried. There was no singing that night.

Still more time passed, extending Joseph's absence by almost three weeks. Lucillus was as much in the dark about the master's return as the family, but he advised everyone that, ship arrivals being extremely unpredictable, there was no cause for concern. At least plans were in place for conveying the expected materials from Caesarea to Sepphoris; there should be no additional delay involved in that. So Joseph could appear at any time.

Reassured but unsatisfied, James kept an anxious eye on Mary. Especially in the latter days, her spirits had seemed to dampen. The nighttime singing had become less frequent, with the sadder tone of her voice dominating, until the songs stopped entirely. Also, she appeared fatigued, and was less and less attentive to Salome's cooking lessons and other chores—so much so that the wives began to suspect that her enthusiasm for learning the domestic arts was waning and perhaps their first suspicions of her unreliability would prove right after all.

One day, Mary was still in her room when James returned from the morning meal at Judas' house. As he was folding the blanket on his sleeping mat, there was a sound of retching. He dropped the blanket, went outside to the stairway, and called up, "Mary, are you ill?"

She was silent. Then James heard the sound of more vomiting.

"Do you need help?" he called again.

Mary appeared at the top of the stairs holding a chamber pot and looking unsteady on her feet. The boy ran quickly up the steps.

"Let me take that," he said. "You are sick. How can I help you?"

"My stomach," she said. "Uneasy for some days. It passes after I lie down."

"I must get Salome."

Mary grabbed the boy's shoulder as he was turning away with the covered container. "No," she said. "I'm alright. Really I am. This will pass. It always does. Say nothing about it to anyone. When your father returns, I will tell him. He will know what to do."

"But Salome might be able—"

"Please, James!" Her voice was emphatic now, pleading. "Say nothing."

The boy looked into her eyes and saw genuine fear. What was it that had so panicked her? He wanted to insist on seeking help, but this picture of desperation made him hesitate to speak.

She repeated quietly but firmly: "Please."

James nodded. He turned, took the pot downstairs and emptied it in the privy.

Mary stayed in her room the rest of that day. She came downstairs only once to seek out some crusts of bread. She had set them aside from the leftovers with the intention of feeding the small birds that came to the sill of her window overlooking a terebinth just beyond the compound wall. Feeling settled now—and hungry—she ate the stale fragments. When she went back onto the portico, she noticed the chamber pot which James had rinsed out and left at the foot of the stairs. She picked it up and carried it back to her room.

That afternoon, James was on his way back from lessons, walking with two other boys who studied with the

Rabbi Ezra. When they reached the square surrounding the town's public well, the other boys broke off and headed for a cobbled alleyway on the far side. James waved to his departing schoolmates and continued on to where the road began its rise up the hill toward his family's compound and then out into the countryside and eventually to Sepphoris.

He was nearly to the gate of his home when he spied some familiar shapes approaching along the road from the opposite direction. The boy's heart leapt at the realization that it was his father walking with Lucillus and the donkey. He ran to Joseph and threw his arms around him.

"Father, oh Father, how I have missed you."

Joseph was knocked slightly off balance and, recovering, laughed as he returned the boy's embrace. "My son," he said. "Surely all of Nazareth will think I had abandoned you."

"I am happy to see you, Father."

"And I you, my son."

As they reached the compound, Josis emerged from the gate. He smiled to witness the boy still clinging to Joseph. "Our scholar has been lonely," he said.

"So it would appear," Joseph said.

Josis went to his father and kissed him on the cheek. "Peace be with you, Father," he continued. "We have all prayed for your safety."

"I am well, as you can see."

"The shipment is received?"

"Partly. The rest is on its way."

"Two other carts are due tomorrow," Lucillus explained.

"Such an elaborate undertaking for a few timbers," Josis

muttered, shaking his head. "These Greeks are so demanding."

"They love their decorative flourishes," Lucillus added. "Every carved leaf or flower petal is savored like a verse of Homer."

"But at such cost," said Josis. "Extra expense in the making, then to ship."

"Plus tolls at the city gates—both Caesarea and Sepphoris," said Joseph.

"The masters of the world grant themselves any indulgence," said Lucillus, taking his leave of the group with a wave and leading his donkey. "Peace be upon the house of Joseph."

They responded to Lucillus' blessing. Then Joseph and his two sons went into the compound, each kissing his own fingers and touching the small scroll. Everyone within rushed to greet the returning patriarch. Except for Mary. When blessings and warm wishes had been exchanged and all were assured that the mission had been completed safely and successfully, Joseph started toward the portico with James at his side.

"I trust Mary is well," he said. "Is she at her prayers?"

"I have not seen Mary since this morning, Father, but..."

The boy's hesitation prompted a flicker of concern. "James?"

"She was sick today, Father. She vomited. I had to clean her chamber pot."

"Sick? Are the wives treating her? They said nothing of it."

"They do not know."

"Why not?"

"Mary forbade me to tell them. She said she has been sick several times but it goes away."

Joseph looked at the boy quizzically, then he turned and went to the portico. James held back to give Mary privacy to explain her illness. Standing at the foot of the stairs, Joseph called, "Mary?"

There was a pause, and then the girl appeared at the top. "Peace be with you, Joseph," she said. "You have returned safely. I am glad."

"James told me you were ill this morning."

"Yes. But I am better now."

"And that you have been ill before."

"Yes."

"You should tell the wives when such things happen. They will care for you. Or one of my daughters can come from—"

Mary interrupted him. "Joseph..."

"Yes?"

"Could you please come up? I would speak with you."

"Of course."

Mary went back into the room as her intended husband began to ascend the stairs. When Joseph came in, he found her seated on a low stool by the rear window. The girl appeared to him as if she were slightly ill even now. Or was she just nervous?

"Yes, Mary?"

Her face was turned away, her eyes closed. "Joseph," she said in a voice barely audible, "something...wonderful...has happened. But it is...difficult...to explain."

Joseph knelt down beside the girl. The way she was seated, with her knees drawn up under her tunic and her arms around her legs, made her look especially small and young—childlike.

"What has happened?"

He watched her. Her eyes were open now, focused on the wall. It was as if she were searching there for words that might serve to make clear a thought that was obscure or subtle. Joseph waited patiently, even as a worry began to come upon him that the girl might be facing a serious threat to her health, about which she hesitated to speak. And yet, whatever it was that had happened she described as wonderful.

"Shortly after you departed for Caesarea," she began, "I was visited."

"Visited? By Hiram, your father's steward?"

"No. Not Hiram."

"Then who?"

"It was a messenger, Joseph."

"From Zacharias—or some other of your father's kinsmen?"

"No."

"From the temple then." He could think of no one else who might send a message to her.

"Not from the temple, or from...relatives..."

Joseph waited. Finally, Mary turned to face him.

"It was a messenger of God, Joseph."

For Mary to use a term so closely linked to the Holy Name itself was unexpected, though perhaps this was a practice among temple girls. How those living within the precincts spoke among themselves was unknown to Joseph. But a messenger of God? Since the days of the prophets, those experiences were considered mainly the stuff of dreams. True visions were rare.

"This came to you in sleep?" he asked her.

"I was awakened from sleep."

Joseph smiled. "As I would have been."

"No, Joseph," she said firmly, seeing his lack of seriousness. "I was awakened from sleep by the messenger. It was then that I saw him and received his message."

Joseph sat now, supporting himself with his hands behind him on the floor and crossing his legs in front. Mary was young, wasn't she? Would an imaginative girl whose childhood had been spent in the temple be inclined toward angelic fancies?

"Mary," he said with fatherly kindness in his voice, "in my dreams I see myself awake. I don't think I have ever dreamed I was sleeping, though surely, one might dream about having just arisen. This is what happened to you."

Her gaze became more sharply focused, penetrating. "I was not dreaming, Joseph. I was visited by a messenger of God, and he told me something wonderful."

In that moment there was complete resolve in her eyes. But then, suddenly, it disappeared, and she turned her face away from her intended husband.

This quick change in her visage set Joseph aback. Girlish dream or no, all he could think to ask her was, "What did this messenger say?"

There was a long pause as Mary contemplated the difficulty of what she was about to divulge. This difficulty was considerable—no, enormous. In fact, she knew that the truth was actually quite unbelievable. And at the same time, she understood that her future, perhaps her very life, depended on Joseph believing it.

After the wait, during which impatience had begun, ever so slightly, to intrude upon Joseph's warmer feeling of fatherly indulgence—the girl turned her eyes back to him. With regained composure and hesitant courage, she framed up her words. "The messenger told me that I am to be the mother of the Son of God."

Joseph's face went slack. Mary, raised in the temple, the very heart of religious life, understood that the words she had just uttered were blasphemy. Indeed, their stunning effect could be read in the blank expression on Joseph's face. Unconsciously his crossed legs stiffened, pressing the edges of his feet against the floor and pushing his body back, away from the girl.

What delusion was this? Was Mary mad? Possessed? Was this what Joachim had meant when he described the intensity of her nature? Had the old man known his daughter harbored such ideas? Was that why she could be placed with no one else? Joseph wished to stop time, to give himself a moment in eternity to make sense of the thoughts coursing through his mind. He didn't know how he should respond to a child who could say such a thing.

And then, somehow, in the midst of a great surge of feeling, the kindness of his heart made him say quietly, "It was a dream, Mary."

She sat without speaking. She looked at this man—this gentle and generous man who had made a heartfelt promise to her dying father—and she knew that her words were turning his act of kindness into an insoluble dilemma. Then tears came to her eyes, because she realized that the explanation of the message she had received was not complete.

She would yet compound his pain and confusion.

"No, Joseph," she said, "it wasn't a dream. What the messenger said was true. I know this is so. I've had only two times of impurity since leaving the temple. The third has not come. And for the past week I have been sick at mornings. I carry a child, the Son of the Living God. The messenger told me I should refer to him as Emmanuel, God with us."

Now Mary was speaking not of dreams, but of observable bodily facts. Even a girl new to the burdens of women would recognize when the blood that should have come did not. And James had verified her sickness. He said he had cleaned the chamber pot of her vomit in the morning, and there could be no mistaking that.

Joseph rose to his feet, his face flushed with anger. That Mary would utter blasphemy was bad enough. That she would offer it to explain away an immoral act was overwhelming deceit.

But still, she was young. She could be prey to a man of low intent. If she did carry a child, who could have done this to her? She had been here in the compound for these weeks, and in her father's house before that, and in Jerusalem before that. And since she said she had passed two times of impurity since leaving the temple, it must have happened while she was here.

Suddenly, he was swept by a horrible wave of guilt. His promise to her father was that he would protect the girl— the treasure of my life, Joachim had called her. Had Joseph failed so miserably at that task? Had Mary really been seduced, led into sin? Had he really been unable to prevent it, so blind as to not even imagine such a possibility, taken no precautions? He could hardly imagine a greater shame.

But who? Who could be responsible for this wicked thing? Joseph would at least know that, and he would take whatever action was necessary.

He turned to the girl again, resuming his kneeling posture before her. "Enough of messengers, Mary," he said sternly. "I do not see God with you in this. Tell me the truth. If you carry a child, whose child is it?"

Mary knew that the truth would not be believed. Yet, there was no other story to tell. What was, was. And in her heart she knew that it was unspeakably glorious, no matter how absurd or shameful it might appear.

Her eyes turned up into the face of this man whom she now feared might never be her husband, and with all her courage and honesty she said, "The Spirit of God came to me, Joseph. The messenger told me it would happen, and it did. I agreed to it. And now I carry the Son of the Living God within me. That is the truth, Joseph, and there is nothing else to say."

Her face, her manner, her voice—the entire presence of this small, childlike creature still on the cusp of womanhood was so disarmingly candid and open that Joseph was not sure if she was actually convinced that this was true, or if nothing had happened at all and Mary's senses had departed from her, or even if he himself was in the grip of a dream.

He struggled to stand again, feeling as if his head was spinning, and set his feet wider to counter the sensation that he might actually fall. When his balance returned, he walked to the door and, without looking back at Mary, went downstairs, passing James in the portico, not even seeing the boy. He entered the lower room now beginning to lose its light with the sun on the down-slope of its daily arc.

Joseph paced about the shadowed space, his undirected steps taking him to the doorway where the sight of James finally registered. That spurred a thought which the family head never would have believed it possible for him to entertain. Could one of his sons have done this to Mary? He recoiled from such a repellent idea, but the thought forced itself into his mind again.

Surely not James. The boy had been in the house with her all these weeks, but James was a mere child. There was not yet the slightest sign that he would even have the capacity.

The others—Josis, Judas or Simon? Could it be? Was it possible? He had raised them to manhood in the way of right and the fear of the Holy One. He knew these three men as he knew himself. It was not possible. He pushed the sordid notion from his mind. "James!" he called.

The boy turned with a start and entered the room, Joseph closing the door after him.

"Tell me, my son, do you know if anyone has visited Mary while I was away?"

"I do not know of anyone, Father," he said.

"Does she walk in the town or the countryside?"

"I don't think so."

"Not in the market street? Not to the well in the square?"

"No," the boy said. "We have our own well."

"Of course. But you are at lessons during the day."

"Yes. But Mary is with the wives then. Salome teaches her to cook."

"She has not gone to the house of Joachim?"

"No one is left there. The servants are gone, the house is empty. I have seen it myself when I've walked by."

Joseph searched his mind, struggling to imagine any possible opportunity for Mary to have met a man. "She has been nowhere?"

"To the synagogue on Sabbath."

"Does she go alone?"

"No. Only with Salome, Zipporah and Sarah. Always with them."

"And she goes nowhere else?"

"No, Father," said the boy, now deeply perplexed by this insistent questioning. "Mary is shy. When she is not with the women, she stays in her room. In the morning she prays, and often at night she sings."

"She sings?"

"Yes. Her voice is nice. I hear her when I'm lying in my bed. I—I enjoy listening to the songs, Father. I hope it isn't wrong."

That shook Joseph out of his agitation for a moment. A fleeting smile crossed his face, and he tenderly rubbed the side of his son's head. "We will speak of this some other time," he said.

But then, new anxieties flashed upon him. If Mary was truly with child, it would become known in the town, and she would be subject to the Law. The girl could be stoned. And just as the thought had crept into his mind that one of his sons might be responsible, that idea could occur to others. The entire family might be in peril.

What he must do was plain to him. He would put Mary aside quietly, end the betrothal in a private way. But first he would get her out of Nazareth.

"James," he said commandingly, "go to Lucillus. Ask him to give you something to eat, and then bring him back here after it is dark."

"But I am supposed to eat at Simon's house tonight."

"Eat with Lucillus. Then have him pack the donkey with supplies for a journey. Bring him back here only when the sun is completely down. And do not come to the gate. Go to the far side of the wall under Mary's window, and call for me there—quietly. I will pack some things for you. You will go with Lucillus."

"I am to travel?"

"Yes."

"But where?"

"You and Lucillus must take Mary to the house of Zacharias."

When James had gone, Joseph resumed his slow pacing about the room. Then he went to find some spare clothes for the boy, and rolled them up into a tight bundle. He took up pacing again, stopping after some minutes when it occurred to him that some explanation would be due Zacharias for Mary's untimely arrival. This should have been obvious, but he had overlooked it in his distress.

He found a small sheet of parchment which had been scraped of previous writing, though not thoroughly, brought it to the low table along with ink and a stylus, and set to writing. The room had become dark, so he lit the oil lamp with a piece of flint struck against a rough stone held at the wick.

Neither time, space, nor circumstance permitted much in the way of form or eloquence, so Joseph made a simple and direct appeal that Zacharias question Mary about a recent apparition. Her answer would make clear why his note was lacking in detail, and also why she was in need of seclusion. He begged the priest's wise counsel as to what steps he, as the girl's intended husband, should take both to satisfy the Law and to fulfill his pledge to Joachim that Mary would never come to harm. And he concluded with an urgent plea for a quick response, which Zacharias could place into the trusted hands of Lucillus.

Holding the parchment near the light, Joseph realized that traces of the earlier message, having to do with a business transaction of some months prior, were still visible under the fresh writing. His message would be plain enough to Zacharias, however, and this would have to do. He rolled up the sheet and tied it with a short piece of leather thong.

Leaving the small scroll on the table, Joseph went outside to the stairway. "Mary," he called to no response.

As he was preparing to go up, there was a sound behind him.

"Father?" It was Zipporah.

Joseph turned with a start.

"James and Mary have not come for the evening meal."

Joseph's hand stroked the side of his face anxiously. "I am sorry, Zipporah," he said. "James has undertaken a task for me. Something unexpected. And Mary is not hungry."

"No one has seen Mary today," Zipporah said. "Is she alright?"

"Yes. Yes. She is fine," Joseph answered, hoping his face reflected his words and not at all certain they had.

"Then...shall I bring you something to eat, Father?" Zipporah asked, less than assured.

"No. Yes. Bring some bread. And some dried figs."

"Surely more than that," she insisted.

"No, just that. And some dried meat."

"Dried meat?"

"Do you have dried meat?"

"Well...yes, but—"

"Dried figs and dried meat, then. And bread."

Zipporah eyed him, bewildered, shook her head, and started across the court to her house.

Joseph climbed the steps and, at the top, peered into Mary's room.

She was kneeling in what appeared to be an attitude of prayer. Through the floor Mary had heard most of what was spoken between Joseph and James. What hadn't reached her ear she inferred, so a stack of clothing sat by the door, wrapped in a blanket and tied up with a cord. Joseph spotted the neat bundle, and he realized that little more would be required in the way of instruction.

"You will leave shortly with James and Lucillus," he said tersely, then went back downstairs.

When Joseph explained to Lucillus that he was to take Mary to Ein Kerem, which was near Jerusalem, Lucillus insisted they should have at least a second man with them.

"This is a long journey," he said, "and brigands are not unknown on those roads. Perhaps one of your older sons might come. Another pair of strong hands and two of Josis' stout gouging axes would be reassuring."

"Axes I can provide," said Joseph, "but all the others in the family must remain here. There are things to be explained which I cannot speak of with them yet. When I have clarity on certain points and the issue about which I have written the honorable Zacharias is resolved, then I will."

This made no sense to Lucillus. Joseph could receive no information until after whoever had gone to Ein Kerem returned. But he could see the master was upset, so he didn't raise the point.

"One of the gang men, then?" Lucillus asked. "How about Nachum? He is strong as an ox. He carries a mortar hod in each hand, and is quick on his feet. And I'm sending him to the sites irregularly just now, so he's available and would appreciate a few extra coins."

Joseph agreed. The party would stop by Nachum's house on the way out of town.

"Another thought, considering safety," Lucillus said. "You know that I love James, and a visit to the famous town of Ein Kerem would no doubt be enriching, but—"

A wave of Joseph's hand cut him off.

"You will be making stops," he said. "You may encounter Roman checkpoints where you'll have to declare yourselves. They set them up unexpectedly, whenever they have word of possible attacks on legion outposts or supply wagons in transit or other troublemaking. And at any place you find lodging—which you will especially need for the Sabbath—a young girl traveling with two men who bear her no relation would raise eyebrows. As for pagan Romans, the crude assumptions that would leap to their minds need not be mentioned. James will represent me. His presence will testify that this journey is a family endeavor."

"But he is only a boy."

"Nevertheless, with him along it will be easier for you to explain that you act on my behalf, taking my intended bride to the home of her kin in preparation for a wedding. You can say I am delayed on business and will follow."

Lucillus' head dipped to one side to acknowledge plausibility in this argument.

"Besides," Joseph continued, "James can stay close to

Mary and shield her from direct inquiries. I do not want her speaking with anyone."

Lucillus' own eyebrows raised.

Joseph gave him a scrip full of gold coins for the journey, and then passed him the scroll he had so hastily prepared. "Give this only into the hands of Zacharias," he said. "And remember, let Mary speak to no one. For that matter, discourage her from speaking even when on the road by yourselves. And if the girl should say anything...strange...please, disregard it."

He gripped Lucillus' arm firmly. "I implore you, my friend," he said pleadingly. "You must trust me. This trip is necessary to protect Mary and to answer a very difficult question. I do not overstate the matter to say it involves life and death."

Lucillus looked deeply into Joseph's eyes and nodded again.

CHAPTER SIX

CONFIRMATION

"Joseph, son of David, do not be afraid to take
Mary your wife into your home."
(Matthew 1)

T he small party made its way through Nazareth, passing in and out of jagged shadows that dissected the moonlight giving the town a pale glow. Beyond the kiln of Reuven the potter, they set out into the countryside on the south road. James led the donkey bearing Mary while Lucillus and Nachum, armed with their walking staves, knives, and Josis' gouging axes, flanked the animal on opposite sides.

Food enough for three or four days travel was stuffed inside leather bags that straddled the donkey's haunches behind where Mary sat wrapped in a heavy cloak against the night chill. Their provisions included the bread, dried meat and dried figs provided by Zipporah, which Joseph insisted they take, even though Lucillus had brought ample supplies.

"The girl must eat," was his cryptic explanation.

Lucillus understood that Joseph wanted Mary away from Nazareth before dawn, but he realized that, starting so late, the party couldn't get far before fatigue overcame them. There was a dense grove set in a hollow some ways out of town and just off the main path, after the road began the first of its step-like descents from the green hills of Galilee.

Tall trees and a thicket of scrub bushes, fed by a narrow stream running from a spring nearby, screened them from view as they spread blankets and took a few hours rest to prepare for the next day's walking.

Shortly after dawn, Lucillus was awakened by the sound of Mary's morning distress. He lay quietly under his blanket as the girl finished and then composed herself, James and Nachum still asleep. He felt confirmed in his suspicions about Joseph's haste to remove her from the scene.

The sun was on its rising arc by the time the party was underway again, but Lucillus accepted the delayed start as a reasonable price for strength renewed. And they would need strength. They made good progress throughout the day, entering into the Jezreel Valley, which the Greeks called the Plain of Esdraelon, a broad and fertile expanse of fields and meadows that cut the nation in half from the coast of the Mediterranean to the valley of the Jordan. That night found them by the River Kishon where several other groups of travelers were camped. The spot was famous as the site of Barak's victory over the army of Jabin and the Canaanite chariots.

Mary had ridden in silence, speaking only once when, with her stomach affected by the pitch and roll of the donkey's gait, she asked to walk. She took her meals similarly without words, except to say the blessings.

For his part, James was completely baffled by the whole situation. He did not understand why Mary had to be taken to the home of her relations, why it was necessary to leave in the middle of the night, or even why he should have been sent along—though he was pleased at the opportunity to visit Ein Kerem, a place he had never been but had heard much about. It was said that the village, near Jerusalem, was so lush and verdant that pomegranates, figs, olives and pears grew wild everywhere. Vineyards bore their fruits without tending. Whether such tales were true he didn't know, but he wished to find out.

The girl's silence was another source of mystery to him. Mary had said so little throughout the day, even though it was apparent to James that the journey was taxing to her. Some words of complaint, or at least an admission of weariness, might be natural. When they were preparing to bed down that evening, he asked if she was feeling alright. She merely smiled at him in a queer and unfathomable way, then turned her face up to the sky and started into what appeared to be a prayer, her lips moving soundlessly. He watched her for some moments sitting in that attitude, then shook his head and laid down to sleep.

The next day brought them to the start of the high road that led up into the hills and through the country of the Samaritans. Nachum expressed distaste for having to traverse infidel lands, common as the route was for those traveling between Galilee and Jerusalem. Lucillus, who had seen much of the world and its various peoples, reminded

Nachum of the hard work Samaritan laborers had provided on several of Joseph's building projects. Nachum granted their strength and industry, but stood by his dislike for these lost cousins of the Jews.

The Samaritan village of Sychar came into view some time later. There they stopped to fill a water skin from the well which Jacob had dug after purchasing the land from the sons of Hamor. Though they could surely have used a rest, Lucillus insisted they press on, knowing that three Jews and a dark-skinned Greek would not be encouraged to linger.

Sustaining themselves on Zipporah's dried figs and meat as they walked, they continued through the high country of Ephraim with the goal of getting as far south of Mount Gerizim as they could. Lucillus considered whether they should attempt to continue walking into the night, since the following day's sunset would mark the start of Sabbath when no travel was possible. The farther they got, the better their chances of finding someplace more welcoming. But Mary was showing signs of weariness and had resumed riding on the donkey's swaying back.

"Are you able to continue?" Lucillus asked her.

She looked at him, and her face took on a strangely peaceful expression, not quite a smile.

"The Lord is my strength and my shield," she said, quoting the psalm. "We will go as far as you think best."

Lucillus nodded. "Let us keep on then," he said.

It was a brave effort, but after several hours of trudging through the dark and cold, Lucillus decided they would have to stop. This was not secure territory, however. They would rest, but he and Nachum would sleep in shifts, taking turns at maintaining a guard. The first watch would be his, he said, at which Nachum objected. Being quite tired himself by now, Lucillus did not resist the big laborer's kindness all that strenuously.

Two hours later, Nachum touched him gently on the shoulder, and the pair traded places. Lucillus watched over the small band until the first pink blush of morning glow. He then woke the others, and the journey resumed.

By the middle of the day they came upon an inn. It was not one of the massive khans that were set along the roads of Judea at regular intervals to service trading caravans and groups of travelers. This was a small lodge that took in the odd wayfarer—really just an out-sized farmhouse—a place where Lucillus had stayed before, run by a farmer whom he knew by name. Arrangements were made to rest through Sabbath. Their arrival was most timely. Mary was exhausted. She fell asleep until James woke her to come to the table where the farmer's wife was preparing to light the Sabbath candles.

Joseph was determined to avoid the questioning eyes of his family. The morning after Mary's departure, he left the compound early and headed for Sepphoris, leaving a note for Josis that he intended to spend the night with one of his foremen. He managed to make that stretch into a second night, but with Sabbath approaching, he knew he would have to return to Nazareth.

He arrived home in mid-afternoon. Salome spotted him in the court and asked if she could bring him some food after his journey. Joseph hesitated at first, but it was now long since he had broken his fast, and hunger forced him to accept some soup and bread. His expression of thanks to her upon its delivery was sincere but terse, almost abrupt.

She asked at which table he intended to take the Sabbath meal, extending an invitation to her own that made him feel somewhat uncomfortable. Joseph knew his presence in one or another of his sons' homes was unavoidable. He accepted Salome's offer with as much good humor as he could muster, and she returned to Sabbath preparations. He was grateful that she had asked no questions about his sojourn in Sepphoris or the unaccounted absence of James and Mary.

Aside from some restrained banter with his granddaughters upon entering Josis' house that evening, Joseph was quiet until he heard the Sabbath trumpet sound its final blast in the distance and Salome lit the candles. Then, as family head, he invoked the three-fold blessing. The meal proceeded with all the awkwardness he had anticipated.

While the family compound had been abuzz with all sorts of speculation, Josis and Salome took particular care not to pry, and their restraint showed. Joseph offered little in the way of casual chatter beyond a recounting of some problems he had been addressing over the past days at the work sites. When the meal was over, he removed himself from the table as quickly as pious practice and common courtesy allowed, returning across the court to his own house.

At this time on the eve of Sabbath, he would normally have immersed himself in prayer in the company of James. But with the boy gone, and under such a cloud of anxiety over Mary's confession, Joseph found it hard to focus on his devotions. He even applied the phylacteries improperly, turning the band that ran down his left arm an insufficient number of times.

He became annoyed at himself over the simple error. But he corrected it and persevered in his recitation of the psalms, eventually gaining a measure of quietude until he was ready for his bed. For all the conflict in his soul, sleep came within minutes of placing his head down. It was a sleep of greater depth and restfulness than any he had known since the death of Escha.

The blackness of the room didn't register on Joseph as he sat bolt upright on his mat, eyes wide open, the grip of his dream suddenly broken but the feelings it had evoked still present. Such a dream! So bright, so vivid, in stark contrast to the deathlike slumber by which he had been consumed until—until the messenger appeared.

Was this what Mary had experienced? If so, it wasn't surprising that she could be convinced she carried a child, even the child of God Himself. This had been enough to shake the heart of a grown man, so naturally, an impressionable young girl would be all the more effected.

But how was it they'd each had dreams so similar—hers announcing the unthinkable and his confirming that it was true? Was this vision merely a trick of the mind? Was it his conscience rebuking him for the harshness he had shown a confused child?

Or was it something else entirely? Something evil? Was it a demon that had come to him—and to her earlier? Such diabolical things were said to happen, even to those of right intent who would never think of dabbling in the realm of spirits.

And yet... And yet...

Mary had insisted it was not a dream, and she'd described the experience as something wonderful. Indeed, this apparition of tonight had left Joseph with the very same feeling. It was wonderful. Clear and vivid and wonderful. Could a demon so thoroughly mislead as to falsely uplift one's soul in such an ecstatic way? It didn't seem possible.

But then, none of this seemed possible.

And yet... And yet...

Joseph was suddenly convinced that what he'd experienced was real, even if, for him, it occurred in sleep, as it surely had. Weren't the holy books replete with tales of prophetic dreams? Even allowing for the rarity of such events, and for Joseph's certainty that he was no prophet, he had to admit that divine communication could happen.

But then what did this imply? Could it be that what Mary had told him was true?

Such a possibility was more than his mind could entertain in the black of night, roused so suddenly from sleep. It was too great and shocking a thought. It was beyond the wildest imaginings. And so he wouldn't consider it now. He couldn't consider it now. No. To the best of his ability, he would set it aside until he was able to speak of it with Mary. And this he would do as quickly as possible.

Yes. He would go after her. Leave now, in the middle of the night. He would run as fast as he could and overtake the party. Or he would reach them at the home of Zacharias. Either way, he would start immediately.

He stood up and groped about the dark room until he

found the flint and stone. He was about to light the oil lamp when he was struck by the realization that it was Sabbath and this would be an impermissible act. He also realized that he would not be able to begin his pursuit until after the next sundown.

Suddenly, Joseph felt horribly torn. He had to speak with Mary. His entire being ached to speak with her. He had to know if the apparitions were genuine. But this was Sabbath, and there could be no travel. He could not leave now. It was the Law.

Still, wasn't it understood that certain urgent needs overrode the Sabbath? Surely, messages from God were of sufficient urgency to preempt the restrictions.

But it was Sabbath, and every fiber of his Jewish manhood argued that the Law must be obeyed.

Joseph felt as if he was being butted back and forth by two huge, angry goats as he pondered this conflict. And then the answer became clear. If the messages were true, then there had been a reason that Mary was given into his care, a reason greater than providing Joachim a peaceful death. The most important thing he was being called to do was to be obedient to the will of the Holy One. And for him to transgress the Law would not be obedience. He had lived by the Law of Moses all his life, and he could not depart from it now. Especially not now.

Hard as it might be—painful as it might be—Joseph would keep the Sabbath.

With the quiet Mary had maintained since leaving Nazareth, James wasn't surprised that she secluded herself throughout Sabbath. She emerged from the small chamber over which Lucillus had haggled amiably with the farmer for her exclusive use—at extra cost—only to take meals.

James wondered at her detachment. At night, lying in the common area on an extremely thin sleeping mat just outside her door, he had thought about her singing upstairs at home. He still wasn't sure if his enjoyment of her songs was entirely appropriate, but he admitted to himself that he missed hearing her voice. Now that Sabbath had passed and they were underway again, the girl remained wordless as she rocked back and forth on the donkey, immersed in her prayers.

But this trip, sudden and unexplained as it was, provided much to distract the boy from thoughts about Mary and her strange silence—the landscape for one. As they approached Jerusalem, James observed how much more sparse and dry the country was than the green hills he knew in Galilee. He had walked this route with his father on previous occasions, but this time he made special note of how the garden plots, vineyards and orchards were largely confined to terraces lining the hillsides, rather than spread out on rolling land as in the north.

He also took interest in the different types of people encountered along the route—Greeks, Samaritans, Idumaeans, Bedouin tribesmen—all on their way to unknown places or converging on the great city of the Jews. At one point, the small party had to step off the road to allow passage of a column of Roman cavalry trotting by in purposeful haste.

Lucillus noted their standards, the crests on the officers' helmets, and the dark, un-Roman faces. "Auxiliaries," he said. "From Libya, I think."

"Pagans!" said Nachum, shaking his head dismissively. "Romans, Greeks, whatever. All foreigners in our land."

Lucillus laughed. "Am I not a Greek?"

"That is what people call you," Nachum said. "But you are not a Greek. You keep the commandments. The pagans laugh at that. They laugh at us. They think we have no religion because we are faithful only to the true Holy One."

"A single god doesn't seem like enough to them," said Lucillus.

"The King of the Universe is enough for anyone— more than enough."

"Well, the foreigners are here, and we build their houses for them."

"I'll take a fool's gold."

Again Lucillus laughed. "They have plenty of it."

"That they do," Nachum said, "lots of gold and lots of gods. I see their home altars. I see how they burn incense to the deities that watch over their grand houses built by Jews. They love all the gods. But what do the gods really mean to them? I think it is all just a show. It is what you do if you are a citizen of the empire. You make sacrifice on Caesar's birthday, and then you go out and get drunk. Some religion."

"Do the pagans not believe in their gods?" James asked.

"Some believe," said Lucillus. "Now it is true that for many the gods and their worship are, as our friend says, just a show. There are hypocrites everywhere. I am told that there are even some Jews who are less pious than they pretend to be. Isn't that so, Nachum?"

"It is. But we Jews do not fill our land with temples and images to make the nations think we are holy."

Lucillus continued smiling at the burly workman. "You

are a philosopher, Nachum," he said, "a student of the human heart." He glanced at James who was looking up at his tutor with questioning eyes.

"I know devotion to the gods can appear false," Lucillus continued, rubbing his face thoughtfully. "But I have known many pagans for whom the divine will is important. And at the heart of it, they admit that all their gods are subject to one supreme divinity. So they are more like the Jews than it might seem. Some sacrifice with great seriousness when their need is great. They follow the auguries diligently when they face a big decision."

Nachum snorted derisively. "What can be seen in the entrails of beasts? Their auguries are meaningless, and their sacrifices are a waste."

"Jews sacrifice."

"We Jews deny ourselves the use of valuable things in recognition that life is a gift from the Creator, the Father of us all. Our sacrifices express our faith."

"As do theirs, my friend," said Lucillus, "in their way. It is not all show, not for those who truly believe. For them it is the root of life. It is what Rome stands for."

The party came over a rise, and the city loomed up in the distance beyond farms, olive groves and clusters of houses scattered across the knolls and hollows that marked the rough terrain before them. Within the grey walls snaking their way around the hill of the Lord, row upon row of tile roofs, interlaced as the threads in woven cloth, rose to a summit. There, shining like some great jewel set at the peak of a diadem, stood the temple.

To James the sight reflected the compact unity spoken of by the psalmist, the place where the tribes came up to give their praise. *I rejoiced when they said we will go to the House of the Lord.* Mary had her own quiet reaction to the sight: a pang of something like homesickness. But the boy felt his heart swell with the excitement that had seized him each time he'd visited the city with his father.

Then, perhaps as a consequence of his age and growing awareness, his eyes were drawn to a set of structures that stood erect and strong adjacent to the temple. These were the four watch towers of the Antonia Fortress. Built by Herod, named for Marcus Antonius, who had been the prime advocate of the Herodian regime, and home to the 600-man Jerusalem garrison, the fortress was a constant reminder of Roman presence and oversight, even of the temple itself. James knew that the ceremonial robes worn by the High Priest were actually kept in the fortress. This was one of many means by which the Romans exerted their control over the nation's religious life, the enthusiasms of which tended to find expression in civil unrest.

"The Greeks and their gods are everywhere, aren't they?" James said.

"They are part of our life," Lucillus answered. "Certainly, they have been part of mine."

"There are some who count the days until we are free of Greeks," Nachum said. "I do."

"Please count them quietly," said Lucillus. "We have to pass the checkpoint at the city gate."

After the sun set on the Sabbath day, Joseph returned to his house from taking the evening meal at Judas' table. He had gotten through Sabbath by maintaining a very uncharacteristic air of reserve, managing to largely avoid speaking about Mary and James. His one vague mention was that the girl had gone to visit her kinsmen and James was accompanying her.

Back in the shadowed lower room, he availed himself of the last faint evening light to gather some things for a trip. He took clean under-linen and rolled it up inside a spare tunic along with his phylacteries and a loaf of bread he had requested from a puzzled Sarah. Then, out of a small recess in the back wall of the room, he retrieved a short Syrian dagger in its scabbard. Finally, he laid down on his mat for a few hours sleep. He would leave with the sun.

In his anticipation of the trip and his continued preoccupation with the vision of last night, Joseph had difficulty getting to sleep. He tossed on the mat for a time, the questions he intended to ask Mary playing over and over in his mind. Eventually he settled into rest, once more to a depth of sleep he would not have thought possible.

The first glow of sunlight woke him, and he rose refreshed to pray an abbreviated version of the morning service without using his phylacteries. Then he put on fresh clothes, inserted the Syrian dagger into his belt next to a small scrip of gold coins, and gathered up the bundle he had prepared for the journey. He went to the door where he put on his sandals and took his walking staff propped against the wall. Going outside, he made a stop at the privy, then went across the court to Josis' house and rapped quietly on the door.

After a moment the face of his eldest son appeared, half awake and confused. "Father?" Josis said. "What is wrong?"

"My son," said Joseph, "I must go to Ein Kerem."

"Ein Kerem?"

"To the home of Zacharias, Mary's kinsman."

"Is that where Mary has gone?"

"Yes. You will have to attend to the building projects in my absence. I am sorry, but...it is urgent that I leave now."

"Of course, Father, but what—"

"All will be explained, my son. Please have trust in me."

"You know I have."

James, Mary and Nachum waited in the shade of some olive trees that stood in lines upon a hill overlooking the junction of roads that paralleled the north and west walls of Jerusalem. One of the city's gates was beyond. The donkey nosed in sparse grass seeking what forage it could. Lucillus had decided it was best not to subject Mary to the prying eyes of the civil guards, or worse, the Roman inspectors who observed all who entered the city, supervised the tolls on freight haulers and caravans, and detained at their discretion anyone who appeared out of the ordinary. So he left the trio at some distance and headed into the city alone.

Some recent incidents of violence had prompted added restrictions on entry. Lucillus was directed to a small side passage which had been set in the blocked gateway, a structure much like the chute through which cattle are driven for culling from the herd, known as the Eye of the Needle. Anyone seeking entry was required to queue up for individual checking and admission. He found himself about twentieth in an impatient line, all of whose occupants were annoyed at the security procedures and the gruff manner of the guards applying them. An amusing exchange between two travelers caught his ear.

"This is how they keep the city safe," said the first, an edge of sarcasm in his voice. "I could bring a camel through this door, and who would know what it carried?"

His companion nodded in agreement. "An extra Caesar's head to the watch, and no one would even ask."

"Well, be grateful for the civil guard," the first friend said. "A temple guard would demand two extra."

Both men laughed. Lucillus smiled quietly.

When he had been admitted, Lucillus went straight to the temple precincts. It had occurred to him that he couldn't be sure Zacharias was to be found at his home in Ein Kerem, not knowing the priestly schedule or what might be required of Mary's kinsman by his business affairs. Zacharias might be at the temple or someplace else in the city. In any event, directions to the priest's home would be helpful, since Joseph had provided none and probably didn't know where the family lived.

In the Court of the Gentiles, Lucillus came upon a priest who knew Zacharias, confirmed that he was not on temple duty at present, and provided the information necessary to locate his house. Lucillus returned to where he had left the others in the olive grove outside the city walls, and after a short rest and the sharing of food from the donkey's pack, the party continued on around Jerusalem to Ein Kerem.

The town was indeed as lush as James had heard, although the orderliness with which the trees and bushes were set and the attention to their care which was clearly evident argued against their springing spontaneously from the earth. Still, the character of the area was a decided contrast with the rest of the gray, rocky country surrounding Jerusalem. James wondered what felicitous combination of soil, rain, breeze and sunshine might account for such plenty.

Zacharias' house was easy to find. It was, in fact, the most imposing structure in the vicinity—a two-story, limestone villa, fronted by a colonnade of fluted posts vaguely suggestive of the temple itself, and surrounded on all sides by its own impressive gardens contained within a wall whose arched gate opened onto the central plaza of the town.

A servant responded to a tug on the bell pull. Lucillus explained that they had brought a kinswoman of the master's wife and that he, himself, bore an urgent message for Zacharias from Joseph of Nazareth, the girl's intended husband. While Nachum remained at the gate with the donkey, the servant led Lucillus, Mary and James to the house, bade the younger two to remain under the shelter of shades that draped from the colonnade, and took Lucillus inside.

Mary found the comfort of a low stone bench, where she sat, tired from the journey, in the silence that had by now become her accustomed mode. James gazed about at the grounds and took several aimless steps, wandering along a side path, and feeling awed by more grandeur than he had ever experienced within a private domain.

After some minutes he heard a sound and turned to see a woman come out of the doorway. Her appearance was a curious mix: a deeply lined face and a head of silver hair, indicating advanced age, along with a clearly defined protrusion at the front. Such a bulge was something one would expect to see only on a much younger woman carrying a child, not on the thin, slightly frail body of this old lady.

Mary rose at her arrival and spoke some words unheard by James, to which the woman reacted with a start, grabbing her belly. James assumed this was Elizabeth, Mary's aunt. And he heard her say something that confused the boy, something about the mother of my Lord coming to her. Then she reached out, took Mary's hands in her own and seemed to bow before the girl.

He went back to the colonnade so that he might be introduced as the son of Joseph, which would be proper in the circumstances. Surprisingly, Mary did not acknowledge his presence. Instead she seemed to be reciting something.

"My soul declares the Lord's greatness..." he heard her say, and she went on at some length, a few of the lines striking James as familiar. He was confused by this display. Perhaps such recitations were a practice of greeting among the members of Mary's family. He couldn't be sure, of course. But when the girl had finished, the older woman's eyes were filled with tears, and she embraced her vigorously.

Inside the house, Lucillus was led to a chamber, the walls of which were lined with shelves, to await the arrival of Zacharias. The servant explained that, while the master would receive him, he was in the grip of a strange malady that had robbed him of his voice. Communication on his part would be by signs and writing, so patience was required.

"He can hear?" Lucillus asked.

"Perfectly," the servant said, turning to leave.

Lucillus waited, his eyes drawn to the numerous scrolls that filled shelves and lay in stacks on other surfaces around the room. His curiosity was aroused, and he wondered what knowledge they might contain.

But his musings were short-lived. Zacharias entered.

"Honored sir, peace be upon you and all your house," Lucillus said, bowing before the famous priest.

Zacharias nodded and then seated himself behind a writing table that bore a tablet of wax held within a frame. There was also a stylus and a small roller with which smoothness could be restored to the wax surface for re-use. He gestured toward a chair, indicating that the visitor should sit.

Lucillus complied, drawing Joseph's parchment from under his cloak. He handed the small wrapped bundle to Zacharias. "From my master, Joseph son of Jacob," he said.

The priest untied the thong and opened the sheet, his eyes making a quick scan of the words. The traces of older writing underscored the urgency with which Joseph had composed his message. Zacharias turned a quizzical eye on Lucillus. Then he set the parchment aside and took the stylus, scratching it into the wax. He held up the tablet for Lucillus to read. "What is it that happened to the girl?" it said in Greek.

"My master was not specific," Lucillus answered tactfully. "But he is much in need of your wisdom. He carries a great burden on his heart."

Zacharias rose to his feet, held up a hand, palm out, indicating that Lucillus should wait, then left the room.

CHAPTER SEVEN

CAUSE FOR REJOICING

*"O the depth of riches both of the wisdom and knowledge of God;
how unsearchable his judgments and inscrutable his ways."*
(Romans 11)

An air of something like rejoicing reigned in the house of Zacharias, which Lucillus, with his suspicions about Mary, found very surprising. Had he misread the situation? Did Mary's morning bouts of illness have a cause other than the presence of a child? If so, why had Joseph been so desperate to remove the girl from Nazareth?

It was clear that neither Mary nor her relatives were inclined to provide any answers, though Elizabeth had conveyed her husband's gracious invitation for Lucillus, James and Nachum to spend the next day resting from their journey before returning to Galilee. Lucillus was profuse in his thanks, but noted Joseph's eagerness for a reply to his message. Elizabeth merely smiled cryptically and expressed confidence that Mary's husband-to-be would be pleased when it came.

One could hardly decline the hospitality of such an exalted family, so the party spent a well fed and comfortable night followed by a further day of relaxation. Nachum found a grassy spot in the garden to enjoy the mild weather of this time in the year. On occasion throughout the day his rest was broken, quite amiably, by the provision of food and wine by the servants. James accepted Zacharias' suggestion, forwarded to him in writing, that the budding scholar might enjoy examining the priest's library. This privilege he shared with Lucillus who, as the boy's tutor, stood by to answer questions and help with any needed translating, since the collection included numerous documents in Greek. Even the donkey basked in the household's luxury, chomping on a seemingly unlimited supply of fodder.

Enjoyable as this respite was in such a magnificent house, enhanced by the pleasant setting of Ein Kerem, Lucillus remained curious, and a bit uneasy, about Mary and about the reaction of Zacharias and Elizabeth to her. He knew of her temple upbringing. Jerusalem was nearby, and Zacharias was a priest. Had the couple been close to her during those years? He would have assumed that the girls of the temple were kept fairly secluded, but he didn't know that for sure.

Then too, there was a certain awkwardness in Lucillus about his social and religious standing, relative to this great keeper of the Law. Judaism prescribed kindness and hospitality to all, even to the alien. And while Lucillus was not quite an alien, he also was not quite a Jew.

He was merely a God-fearing gentile whose attendance at synagogue was regular but who did not bear the mark of the Covenant in his flesh. Even if the kindness of this priest was abundant, Lucillus did not feel entirely at ease.

James, on the other hand, was enthralled by this experience. While the reason for their trip remained a mystery to him, he was grateful for the opportunity to glimpse the home and daily doings of a leading religious figure—one who had held out the promise of entry into the inner circle of scholarly life. His mind was alive with the observations he would share with the Rabbi Ezra, and it stoked his eagerness for the day of his reading in the synagogue and the attainment of his maturity.

Throughout the afternoon Mary was the sole focus of her relatives' attention. Elizabeth had a divan carried out to the garden, over which the servants assembled a small pavilion of wicker screens. She insisted that the girl recline, ordered refreshments brought to her continuously, and peppered her with solicitous questions about her comfort and contentment. At one point, feeling rather dazzled by such fuss, Mary burst out laughing. James, who happened to be standing in the colonnade, noted her amusement, which pleased him after the days of silence.

Meanwhile, Zacharias came to the garden repeatedly with questions written out on parchment or scribed into the wax tablet. At various times both James and Lucillus saw the girl speaking to him at length, apparently answering his inquiries, the old man's head nodding solemnly. All of this seemed more than mere indulgence of a favorite niece. These exchanges held a significance, which James and Lucillus detected but could not understand.

Finally, that evening as Lucillus was preparing for sleep, Lemuel, the steward of Zacharias' house came to him bearing a scroll tucked inside a linen pouch. Both the scroll and the draw strings of its container were closed with wax seals bearing the signet of Zacharias.

"A message for Joseph of Nazareth," the steward said. "My master wishes you a safe and swift journey as you depart in the morning. He prays for your protection and offers his blessing upon the much favored house of Joseph."

"Please convey to him deepest gratitude for the great hospitality he has shown my companions and myself. May peace be upon the house of Zacharias."

At first light, Lucillus, James and Nachum were assembled by the front gate, Nachum loading the donkey with provisions for the journey brought out by a servant girl. They were about to depart when Mary appeared in the colonnade. She came across the garden to them.

"Thank you," she said, "for bringing me safely to the home of my relations. May the Holy One of Israel watch over you and keep you in His care." Then she said specifically to James, "Please convey my respect and affection to your father. Tell him I await his arrival eagerly."

"Yes, Mary," the boy answered. "I will tell him. Be well. I hope we will see you again soon. Peace be upon you."

While James accepted Mary's words as a simple parting sentiment, Lucillus took note of her expression of eagerness for Joseph's arrival.

Was she merely stating her hope to see him again at some undetermined time in the future? If she did carry a child, who knew when that might be—if ever? On the other hand, could her words refer to something in Zacharias' well-sealed message? Had the priest made a special appeal for Joseph to come? Was Joseph's presence somehow demanded? Questions heaped upon questions.

They set out on the road back to Jerusalem, James at

pains to take in every view of the fertile haven they were departing. At one point, standing on a rise, he looked back and noted the contrast between the district of Ein Kerem and the surrounding countryside, which changed markedly over a very short distance. By the time they were again outside Jerusalem, rocky soil and sparseness of vegetation were the predominant features.

But there was no ignoring the dramatic presence of the great city. As they passed its walls, the boy felt once more a thrill of anticipation at the prospect of studying with the doctors of the Law. What arrangement would Zacharias make for him? And what might such an opportunity portend for his future?

He was deep in his thoughts about great things to come when Nachum called out, "It is the master."

Lucillus looked up. "Hmm?"

"Joseph. It is Joseph," the big laborer said, pointing forward.

James spotted him now. "Yes. It is Father!" The boy ran to him, Joseph taking his son in his arms.

"Peace be upon you, Joseph," Lucillus said when they had caught up. "But what are you doing here? I thought you wanted us to—"

"You have done well, my trusted friends," Joseph said, "everything I asked. But I received some additional information after you left, and it became necessary for me to make the journey myself."

"I am happy to see you, Father."

Joseph rubbed the side of the boy's head in his fatherly way. "And I you, my son." Then to Lucillus: "How was Mary received?"

"Remarkably well."

"And my message to Zacharias?"

"Whatever it was that you told him, his fervor over this kinswoman only increases the longer she is there.

Joseph nodded his head and smiled. "Has he told you anything?"

"Zacharias tells no one anything," Lucillus said. "Some malady blocks him from speaking."

"The illness persists?"

"He writes messages, Father," said James.

"And Mary? She has said nothing?"

"Other than a few words of thanks at our departure," Lucillus replied, "she kept the silence of the sphinx during the entire journey. She does speak with Zacharias and his wife, but we don't know what about."

"Mary is happy to be there, Father."

"With good reason," said Lucillus. "They treat her like your great ancestor would have treated the Queen of Sheba."

Again Joseph smiled. "Well, my friends," he said. "You must return with me to Ein Kerem." He patted the donkey on a haunch and gestured for the three to follow.

"Fine with me," said Nachum. "The house of Zacharias is a comfortable place."

"Shouldn't we get back to Nazareth?" Lucillus asked. "The projects."

"Josis has everything in hand, I'm sure," said Joseph over his shoulder. "I have important words to share with Mary." And he set a brisk pace, the others falling in behind.

James quickened his steps to parallel Joseph's stride. "Father, a very interesting thing did happen when we arrived."

"Oh?"

"When Mary was greeting her kinswoman, Elizabeth, she recited something. It was quite long, and at first I thought it was the Song of Hannah. At least it sounded something like that. But Mary said it in a different way and changed things. I never heard anyone give a recitation when they were greeting someone."

"Did Elizabeth recite anything back to her?"

"No, but she looked very excited about what Mary was saying." The boy scratched his head. "What could it have meant, Father?"

"I do not know. But unexpected things can happen, my son, many unexpected things."

Then Lucillus said, "Zacharias has given me a reply to your message." He handed over the sealed pouch containing the scroll. "You may wish to read it before you see him."

Joseph took the package, then stopped and said, "Yes. Everyone rest for a while. I will have a look at Zacharias' words."

He found a large rock off to the side of the road, deposited himself on it, snapped the wax tab that held the drawstrings together, and opened the pouch. Then he broke the seal on the scroll and read the priest's message as the others watched from a distance. Lucillus studied Joseph's face and observed his visage turn from curiosity to what seemed a look of deep satisfaction. He saw Joseph close his eyes and begin to rock forward and backward, mouthing words silently as in prayer.

What has come upon this family? the Greek asked himself in his thoughts.

Mary's face lit up at the sight of Joseph walking across the garden to where Elizabeth had her ensconced on the divan once more, shaded by the wicker panels. The girl rose to her feet. She and her intended husband shared a knowing smile as the distance between them closed.

"Peace be with you, Joseph," she said.

"Peace be with you, Mary."

"Do you know now?"

"The messenger came to me."

"And you believe?"

"I cannot think it otherwise than real."

"It is real."

"The marriage must take place at once," he said. "We cannot let any more time go by. People will make their calculations, and there must be no basis on which questions can be raised. The child's place in the family and in the synagogue must be secure."

"Yes, Joseph. Zacharias can arrange it."

"Is he not ill?"

"No, merely lost his voice. The Holy One has touched him—and touched Elizabeth as well."

"So he said in his message." Joseph gazed off toward the sky, then back at Mary, and then down at the ground. His head turned slowly from side to side. "But I must confess, I do not understand."

"We have all been chosen, Joseph," she said. "We have been chosen by God."

———

Joseph sat beside Zacharias on a bench in the garden from late morning until well into the afternoon, their conversation hampered by the priest's need to write out his words on the wax tablet in his lap.

But eventually they worked out a plan for the wedding, which would be conducted in private within the next few days.

Since Zacharias would be unable to speak the marriage blessings, he sent his steward to Jerusalem with instructions to seek out Simeon, a scribe of advanced age and great holiness. With the decline in his physical capacities, Simeon spent most of his time in the temple praying for the consolation of Israel.

"He is a friend of many years," Zacharias wrote on the tablet, "pious and discreet."

Arrangements would have to be made to convey Simeon to Ein Kerem. "It will not be easy for one so infirm," Zacharias wrote, Joseph following the scratching of the stylus. "But I believe he will be eager to do it when I make the situation clear." He drew the roller across the wax, smoothing the surface, and then inscribed, "It will accord with certain assurances which he says he has received in his prayers."

"How much can we take him into our confidence?" Joseph asked "There is risk in speaking of the messages we have received."

Zacharias nodded and then wrote, "Simeon is one of very few people whom I would trust to understand." Then, after rolling the surface clean again: "I believe this may be what he has waited for."

A litter carrying Simeon arrived late the next day. The frail form, crowned with wisps of feathery white hair, hardly seemed to require the combined strength of the four husky lads whom Lemuel had hired to bear it. But the old man's eyes were bright, his mind sharp. Immediately upon being helped from the chair, he began questioning Zacharias as to what was this exciting purpose of the Lord to which the priest's message had alluded.

Zacharias took him by the hand and led him into the house where he and Joseph shared the story of Mary's and Elizabeth's conceptions, the confirmations which the two men had received, and the role which Simeon was being called upon to play.

The old scribe sat quietly for some time, lost in a kind of wonder. It all came back to him—the conviction, felt over and over again as a promise from the Lord Himself that Simeon should not die until he had seen the Anointed One with his own eyes. He was convinced of it. He lived for that day alone.

Finally, he asked that Mary be brought to him. When the girl came in, he looked her up and down, slowly and carefully, as if assessing her worthiness for such an unimaginably important task as Joseph and Zacharias claimed she had been given.

She was so young, only just beyond childhood. And lovely. In the earliest blush of womanly ripeness, like an offering of first fruits. He considered the facts of her life: of a priestly clan, raised in the temple—he thought he recognized her from the precincts—her entire being dedicated to the Holy One of Israel. Surely, this was one such as the Lord would choose.

Perfect.

"You must promise that I can see this child," he said. "Alert me when you bring him to the temple."

Mary nodded, her eyes turned demurely to the floor. "You have my promise, sir," she answered.

"Then yes, I will conduct the wedding," said Simeon.

Zacharias and Simeon gave extensive consideration to whether Mary should go to the synagogue in Ein Kerem for the ritual bath normally required of a woman before her wedding. With the unprecedented circumstances of this particular wedding, neither the priest nor the scribe felt certain how the prescriptions of the Law would apply. Concerns about impurity associated with the female cycle seemed of less urgency since Mary and Joseph were beginning their married life without the expectation of normal marital relations. Their standing toward one another would necessarily be different from that of most husbands and wives. What were the ritual implications of that? Then too, didn't the fact that Mary carried the Child of the Most High suggest purity in the eyes of Heaven? Who could be more immaculate than she who was chosen to be the Lord's vessel?

Still, the Law had its obligations. In the end they judged that a ritual bath was, if not required, then certainly appropriate. Joseph too was certain he should purify himself, called as he was to be the guardian of this special child.

While the wedding would be conducted as inconspicuously as possible, Elizabeth insisted that some effort be made to create a festive atmosphere. She had the servants bring flowers from the garden to decorate the villa's common room. She arranged a special feast for those who would be in attendance: Mary and Joseph, along with James, Lucillus and Nachum, and of course, Simeon,

Zacharias and herself. And she rigged a wedding canopy, using a large, ornate prayer shawl suspended from the tops of four poles. There might be no procession through the streets. No one would sing from the Song of Songs. But this would still be a celebration.

Her efforts were worthwhile—and successful. The wedding was joyous, if small and somewhat subdued. Mary beamed with the radiance of all brides, her youth and innocent beauty touching everyone in attendance, especially James. Perhaps for the first time, a suggestion of future joy —the joy which only life with a woman can offer— insinuated itself into his youthful heart. In a way which he did not fully understand, he felt himself envying his father.

By now it was clear to Lucillus, Nachum and, to an extent, James as well, that something extraordinary was happening. The hasty conveyance of Mary, the unexpected appearance of Joseph, the hushed consultations, the secretive wedding arrangements—everything suggested important, though hidden, motives. Lucillus especially, the worldly-wise Greek who kept his own counsel and who knew his employer as the most upright of men, was convinced that Mary was with child and that Joseph had decided to take her as his wife anyway.

But why? What conditions would prompt such an act? Lucillus understood the Jews and their fierce moral scruples. Something more was at work than Joseph's kindness or his commitment to honor a promise to Mary's father. Lucillus watched the ceremony unfold, he listened to the pledges and blessings, and he wondered. He wondered.

Very little seemed to have changed in the days after the wedding. Mary maintained her repose out in the garden, lying on the divan, as insisted upon by Elizabeth. And the furtive consultations continued, now between Mary, Zacharias, and Joseph. Nachum, in particular, found it all very perplexing. While he had deduced Mary's condition, it was nonetheless strange to him that the bride and groom were not even sharing a bed chamber. If their behavior toward one another during the day embodied respect, even modest affection, the pair sought no privacy. It was hardly what one would expect of newlyweds, even newlyweds of such different ages.

He spoke his thoughts on the matter to Lucillus who took it upon himself to explain the agreement between Joseph and Joachim, of blessed memory, as the master had confided it during their sojourn in Caesarea. Lucillus felt it best to nip Nachum's speculations in the bud, and he obtained a pledge that this information would go no further.

"I am not a gossip," the big laborer said with a hint of indignation.

When the time came to depart for Nazareth, Joseph asked Zacharias if Mary might remain in Ein Kerem for a time. Reflecting on the discord that had attended Mary's initial introduction into his household, he felt it wise to bring the rest of his family to some understanding of the situation before her return. That the Holy One had called this family to the honor of His service was a challenging enough idea. The divine origin of Mary's condition would be even less readily accepted. A bit of time might be needed for the facts to settle upon everyone's hearts, and it was essential that they did so. Zacharias agreed.

For her part, Mary thought that remaining at the villa might actually be an advantage, the closer Elizabeth got to the birth of her own child—that is if Elizabeth would stop fussing and let her help. She suggested that she stay at least until Elizabeth's delivery, around Passover. Zacharias expressed his appreciation to her, and indicated that he would convince his wife to accept Mary's assistance.

And so, the morning after the first Sabbath following the wedding, Joseph departed Ein Kerem with James, Lucillus and Nachum, leaving Mary behind.

CHAPTER EIGHT

PAINFUL ANNOUNCEMENTS

"I will be with you as you speak,
and I will instruct you in what to say."
(Exodus 4)

S ome inconsistencies were discovered in the carved beams brought from Lebanon. Several had not been cut precisely to specifications. Adjustments made to install them resulted in slight irregularities of appearance, which did not please the Greek client whose house was being built. Consequently, Josis had spent much of the two weeks since Joseph's departure in Sepphoris figuring out ways to disguise the flaws and placating a disgruntled customer.

"Shoddy Jew work," was the phrase that rang in his ears during several difficult negotiating sessions. Josis explained to the client, a mid-level official of the Roman civil administration, that the errors had been made in Lebanon, not by his Jewish craftsmen. In the end, he had to commit, on behalf of his father, to an adjustment in the fee for the entire building project, which restored some measure of grudging contentment. But with such distractions in Sepphoris and carpentry jobs piling up again in Josis' workshop, it was with extra joy that Joseph was greeted by his eldest son upon returning to the family compound.

"Peace be with you, Father. You should know how eagerly I thank heaven for your return."

Joseph had to smile. "I suspect there is more in this than the love of a loyal son."

"There is, Father," said Josis. "You are much needed." And he explained the problem with the beams, expressing his hope that he had done right in making adjustments to the fee.

"Was the customer satisfied in the end?" Joseph asked.

"More than he wished me to know, I think." said Josis. "Later that day I overheard him saying how the irregularities in the woodwork seemed to give his house more character."

"And saved him money," said Joseph, laughing. "You did what was necessary, my son."

Then, in a more subdued tone, Joseph asked Josis' assistance in organizing a meeting of the adults in the family, his sons and daughters and their spouses. "Mary and I have married," he told his son.

"Married? Where? When?"

"In Ein Kerem. And she has remained in the house of Zacharias to be of aid until her kinswoman, Elizabeth, delivers," he said.

"But why did you marry there, Father, without the family present?"

"I will explain all when everyone is assembled. And

much more as well. There are things which they must know before Mary returns."

"What things, Father?"

"In time, Josis. In time. But please appreciate that this bears on the safety and the future of the entire family."

"As you wish, Father," Josis said. "I will speak with them."

It took two days for Josis to assemble everyone, during which time Joseph removed himself to Sepphoris from early morning to late at night, hoping to avoid inquiries he was not yet prepared to address. With his father gone, James became the focus of curiosity, especially among his sisters-in-law. Joseph had said nothing to indicate that the marriage should not be spoken of, so the boy did his best to answer their questions about the wedding. Why had it taken place so suddenly, and why in Ein Kerem, and why in such a private manner?

"It was how Father wanted it," James said with a shrug. "He had many long conversations with Zacharias. I suppose this was what they thought best. And the ceremony was very nice. Lots of flowers."

But why had Mary stayed behind? All understood that she would not be a wife to Joseph in the usual sense. Nonetheless, it seemed odd that a newly married woman should separate herself in this way. Would she not attend to her husband? Was his care to remain the responsibility of the other wives? Was this yet another sign of the queer presumptions one might expect of a temple girl?

James felt the women had leapt to conclusions that were very unfair to Mary. But events had unfolded so quickly and unexpectedly, and the air of mystery that surrounded the wedding was undeniable. He really had nothing with which

to allay their suspicions. If only his father would come forth
with an explanation that could answer everyone's questions,
including his own.

The day of the family meeting Joseph spent extra time
in the synagogue after the morning service. He prayed
silently that he be given the words to convey this difficult
story to his household with conviction and persuasiveness.
All depended upon his being believed, and he didn't doubt
for a minute the unbelievable nature of what he had to say.
Unless others had received revelations similar to his own—
and he harbored no illusions that anyone had—the onus
was on him to make them accept that the Holy One of
Israel had chosen this family, alone among all the clans of
the Jews, for His own special purpose. Only then could they
accept the child Mary was carrying and the circumstances
under which she had conceived.

Upright as he was, Joseph might equivocate with those
outside the family—let them assume what they would—but
he could not lie to his own. To claim that the child was his
would make it appear that he had violated his pledge to
Joachim and maybe even forced himself upon an innocent
girl placed under his protection. Likewise, to assert that
Mary had changed her mind, abandoned a commitment
that supposedly had been so strong as to induce her father
to make this highly unusual contract, would say nothing
good about her steadiness of purpose. Finally, and most
important of all, Joseph could not permit anyone to believe
that his wife had sinned before marriage. That would be
unthinkable.

Such was the dilemma that occupied Joseph as he left
the synagogue, heading toward the family compound. He
searched his memory for a passage of holy writing which he

might pray in preparation for the difficult task ahead. But nothing that came to mind seemed quite relevant to his situation. Closest was the psalm that offered assurance that a man could dwell in the tent of the Lord if he was truthful and kept a promise even when it was painful to do so.

When he reached his house, the gate was ajar. He touched the scroll and went inside. He could see that all the adults were present, sitting or standing in the portico. Except for James, who stood with his brothers, the children were all gathered at the far end of the court by the entrance to Josis' house, the older ones looking after the younger as Josis had insisted. There were more children than usual, since his daughters had brought theirs.

Enoch, the husband of Joseph's daughter, Assia, raised a hand in greeting. "Peace be with you, Father Joseph," he called.

"And upon all of you," Joseph replied. "I am most grateful you have come." He strode into the portico, giving a nod to Jubal, husband of daughter Lydia. "There are important things to speak about."

His sons had carried an assortment of stools and benches to the portico. The Roman-style chair that had come from Joachim's house was placed in a position of prominence. Assuming it was meant for him, Joseph sat on it as the others arranged themselves, the men on one side, women on the opposite. He looked about at each of his sons and daughters and their spouses, his eyes proceeding from face to face. While nothing was said, he could read curiosity, even anxiety, in their attentive expressions.

"My children," he began, "I know you are confused about events of recent days. I am sorry to withhold my explanation, but I felt that informing you all together was the only fair way."

This drew nods of assent, which Joseph found encouraging. Strangely, though he was head of the family and they his children, at this moment he felt very much like a child called upon to deliver a message he did not fully comprehend to a group of adults unlikely to take him seriously. It made him feel distinctly unsettled.

Then a passage from Jeremiah came to his mind: The Lord said to me, "Do not say, 'I am a child,' for to whomever I send you, you shall go, and whatever I command you, you shall speak. Do not be afraid of them, for I am with you to deliver you." He pondered the line for a moment, drew a breath, and continued.

"What I have to tell you is not easily understood," he said. "And I think that your acceptance of it will require more than mere trust in me."

This raised concern in several hearts, because Joseph held a position of utmost respect among all present. His two sons-in-law considered themselves—and were thought of throughout the town—as the most fortunate of men to have married the carpenter's daughters. And their trust in him had been vindicated on more than one occasion.

"Rather," Joseph continued, "I ask you to listen to me and consider what I have to say...as Jews."

Was there to be some sort of religious pronouncement? Perhaps having to do with the strange circumstance of the wedding? What was he about to tell them?

"We are fortunate—we Jews—not to be burdened with so many legends and fantastic tales, such as those the pagans are told. We are not raised on wild stories of the gods and their antics, their struggles and tragedies, their immoral delights, their dalliances with mortal women, and all the other nonsense by which the Greeks are so rapt."

Joseph's family had been amused by his comments on pagan folly before. He could speak with authority, having so many dealings in Sepphoris. This reflection brought smiles of familiarity to several faces in the group.

"Jews, on the other hand, are asked to believe very little, compared with the vast array of Greek myths. We know that all comes from the Creator of the Universe and it is His hand that guides our lives. Our fate is not at the mercy of flawed beings whose character is no better than our own and whose whims we must placate. The Lord is our shepherd."

Joseph's forthright manner of speaking sparked a thought within James, which the boy had entertained before: If his father's life had been different, he would have made an excellent rabbi. Clearly, this was the fount of James' own inclinations. If he could take full advantage of the opportunities promised by Zacharias, perhaps he could be the scholar Joseph should have been.

"And yet," Joseph continued, "there are certain things we are given to believe as Jews, things which are not the stuff of everyday experience. For instance, that Moses parted the sea so that the Children of Israel could escape from bondage in Egypt. Or that the lamp burned brightly for eight days in the temple, even though the oil was insufficient. These things are recorded, and we accept them, because we know the hand of the Holy One is in them. Yet they are extraordinary. It is because they are extraordinary that they have meaning to us and we celebrate them."

He paused, offered a quick, silent prayer for courage,

and then went on. "I would ask you all...as Jews...to believe that something—that something similarly extraordinary—has happened within our family."

There was a stirring throughout the group, but no one said anything.

How to approach this? Joseph decided that he would start with his own experience and then work back to the more daunting situation of Mary. "I have had a vision," he said. "It came to me in a dream, but I know in my heart it was more than a dream. I was visited by...the Lord's messenger."

Another stirring. No one now doubted that what Joseph wished to tell them was worthy of the suspense he had fostered. But this was their father, a man of pious devotion, yes, but a practical man of business as well, and not one given to vain spiritual imaginings.

Joseph explained further: "This happened after my return from Caesarea. And it came in the way of...confirmation...of a still earlier event. You see...Mary had told me that she too...had been visited. And the message she received...and which she conveyed to me...was disturbing. Shocking, actually."

He paused again, briefly, but did not allow hesitancy to take hold.

"It was because of what she said that I sent her away. I needed time to reflect on what her words would require of me. But after she departed...the messenger came again. And he assured me that what Mary told me was true. As unbelievable as it might be...it was true."

Still another pause, longer this time. Everyone watching Joseph's face could see deep unease in his expression, though they did not know its cause. They did not know that it was prompted by raw fear at having to make this revelation to those who had not shared his experience.

After an awkward silence, James, with the impatience of his age, spoke up for the group. "What did Mary tell you, Father?"

Joseph glanced at his youngest son. Of course it would be James to ask. Endlessly curious James. Then Joseph's eyes swept the group again, from face to face, finally settling on his own hands clasped in his lap.

"She told me that she had conceived the child of the Holy Spirit—Emmanuel...God with us."

Backs stiffened all around the portico. Joseph was right to have been shocked and disturbed. Zipporah rose to her feet.

"Mary spoke...blasphemy...Father," she said. "Such an idea... To say this thing—to even think it—a temple girl... This— This is— And you married her?"

Joseph's eyes were closed now. He knew the thoughts tearing at everyone's minds. They were all of the thoughts he'd had himself.

"Yes. I married her."

"But how— How could you?"

Simon rose and walked across the portico to his wife. "Zipporah," he said, touching her on the arm. Then, self-conscious in front of the others, he drew his hand away. "We will hear Father's answer."

Joseph looked up at his daughter-in-law. "I married Mary because what she said was true."

Zipporah's face was blank with disbelief, her expression not unlike that of the others. Silence fell over the group again until, after some seconds, Josis spoke.

"Father," he asked, "is Mary with child?"

"Yes."

"And you are convinced that her explanation for this is true?"

"Yes, I am," said Joseph, his eyes now trained directly on his eldest son. "I was not...not at first. When she told me these things I reacted much as Zipporah has. I was confused, and I was angry. And I was... I was guilty."

"Guilty?" Josis asked, incredulous. "You, guilty?"

Joseph nodded. "I felt I had failed in fulfilling my promise to her father. I had gone away to Caesarea and left her in Nazareth. I had not kept her from harm."

Josis was without a thought of how to respond, and there was another awkward, wordless moment.

Then Joseph spoke again. "I determined to put her aside...to end our betrothal with no public declaration...and to let her relatives care for her. I thought that by removing her quickly to Ein Kerem I could at least shield her from public disgrace here and— Well...I would not expose her to the Law if the sin was found out."

"But the sin is found out."

"Zipporah!" Simon said sharply.

"There is no sin," said Joseph. "My vision has confirmed this. The messenger assured me that Mary told the truth. The Spirit of the Lord came to her, and she conceived. No earthly man was involved. Her child is...the Son of the Living God."

At these words a collective gasp was heard across the portico. Could their father, the devout and revered Joseph, be telling them that the King of the Universe Himself had chosen to make this household his own? That this girl who had come into their midst so unexpectedly was to bear a divine child? Such ideas were not only blasphemous, they were absurd. They were things only pagans could believe. Had their father spent too much time among the Greeks? Had he lost his mind?

Josis looked at this man who had raised him, loved him, taught him his life's craft, and he struggled to give the benefit of the doubt to what he had just heard. "I do not see how this can be, Father," he said gently. "Are you...certain...Mary is not lying? And that this confirmation was...real?"

All the others waited for Joseph's response, hoping for—what? That he would recant? That he would offer some proof? No one knew quite what it was they did expect.

Joseph took his time before answering Josis' question. He grappled for just the right set of words with which to take hold of his children's hearts, to inspire them with his conviction. He searched and he prayed.

But before he could speak, James stood up.

"I believe you, Father," he said.

Zipporah turned and glared at him. "James, you are just a child," she said.

At this the boy's face flushed deeply. "I saw with my own eyes that Zacharias and Elizabeth believe." The reply to his sister-in-law had an assertiveness that surpassed his years. "Zacharias and Elizabeth rejoiced when Mary arrived. Elizabeth called her 'the mother of my Lord.' Why would she call her that? They embraced Mary, waited on her hand and foot as if she were a queen. And Zacharias is a holy man, a priest of the temple."

Joseph cast a sideward glance at the boy, and a faint smile crossed his lips. Dear James.

Then a word of support came from an unexpected source, the usually quiet Judas. "If we believe that the Holy

One spoke to the prophets," he said, "can we not consider that our father might receive His message?"

Another pause, and then a comment from Assia's husband, Enoch: "Brother Judas has a point," he said. "The righteousness of Joseph the Builder is known throughout all of Galilee. If the Holy One were to send a child into this world, why not put him into the care of our father? Besides, do not all Jews pray that Messiah might come?"

Jubal, Lydia's husband, gave a quick, wry laugh at the mention of the Deliverer. "We have seen messiahs before, brother," he said, "and much tragedy to follow them. Many vain hopes have been raised, and much blood spilt."

"True enough," Enoch said. "But who knows for what purpose someone might be sent from on high?"

There was silence again. Then Josis said, "Judas and Enoch speak wisely. And James has reported what he witnessed for himself. Messiah or not, if this is the Lord's work, we will see the evidence in due time. We must be patient and wait for Him to reveal it."

Josis paused, understanding clearly now the reason for the haste of the wedding and for Mary not returning with her husband. "In the meantime," he continued, his voice bearing the authority of the eldest son, "we know our father, and we stand by him. Moreover, Mary is his wife, so we will welcome her when she returns to us." Then he added with a meaningful glance all around, "Of course... this remains inside the family."

It could hardly be said that all were satisfied with Joseph's story. But most decided to withhold judgment on the man they knew so well and respected so highly. They would follow Josis' lead as best they could, waiting with as open a mind as possible.

This did not mean they were without doubts and questions. Zipporah especially felt the tug of conflicted feelings. She confided her anxiety to Salome and Sarah that Joseph's vision might be less a confirmation of Mary's claim than a troubling sign of advancing age with greater confusion yet to come. If that was the case, then what new burdens might fall on the wives? With a divine child to command her attention, would Mary even concern herself with the well being of her much-older husband?

Mary. This was Joseph's main concern right now. He realized that, if Mary's entry into the family had been contentious, her return, in present circumstance, promised even greater discord. Perhaps to crisis proportions, if Zipporah's feelings were any indication. He hoped that Mary's sojourn in Ein Kerem would provide time for the shock of his disclosure to subside. Elizabeth still had many weeks before her child was due, though at that point Mary's physical appearance would likely reveal her own state. Well, nothing to be done about that. At least everyone would be prepared for what, when she next appeared, would probably be quite conspicuous.

In the emotion of the family meeting, Joseph had not thought to relate what Zacharias and Elizabeth told him they believed about their own child, who was coming to them under extraordinary circumstances as well. They had received their own visions announcing Elizabeth's conceiving in old age. It was because Zacharias had expressed doubt at the possibility of such a thing that his voice had been taken from him. At least, that was what they believed. Now they were convinced that their child had a role to play as a herald of Mary's. If they were correct, then surely this provided some validation of the visions Joseph and Mary had experienced.

But no. Perhaps it was just as well he hadn't mentioned any of that. Perhaps it would have been too much, made the whole situation seem even more fantastic. To convey these things might merely have raised questions about Zacharias and Elizabeth. Joseph's children might assume that Mary's entire family was deluded. Or possessed. Better this drama unfolded gradually, one step at a time.

The immediate question—the one to be addressed over the coming weeks—was how to bring everyone in the household into agreement with Josis' promise that they would welcome Mary. This would be a test of Joseph's claim on their loyalty and confidence in him.

James had returned from Ein Kerem bubbling over with all he had seen and eager to discuss it. The first day back in class he shared his observations about the surprising lushness of the district, spoke of his excitement at being in the home of the famous priest, and described the remarkable documents he had perused in Zacharias' library. While the other boys found the report of his adventure modestly engaging, the Rabbi Ezra was deeply intrigued.

After the classmates were gone, James and his teacher discussed Joseph's wedding. Ezra was surprised to hear of the suddenness with which this sacred function had been carried out. His curiosity was piqued, and there was the slightest trace of professional disappointment, since he had assumed that he would officiate in binding Joseph to the daughter of Joachim. Still, he was most interested in the boy's animated recounting of the affair.

The morning after the family meeting, however, James' attitude was entirely changed. With his father's revelation of what had been behind the wedding and his eldest brother's insistence on strict confidentiality, the boy felt inhibited in speaking about anything related to the trip.

Ezra noted this sudden reticence, so much in contrast with the previous day. He didn't probe him on it, but he got the distinct impression that James' enthusiasm had been intentionally curtailed. All of which added to the strangeness of this abrupt turn which Joseph's betrothal to Mary had taken, raising questions in the rabbi's mind.

Why was it done this way? The wedding of a man with the prominence of Joseph would surely be an occasion for the whole community to celebrate. And Mary's status as daughter of the wealthy landowner—even with her father passed away—would give the event even greater significance, the coming together of two leading families of Nazareth.

No doubt Joseph understood the importance of that to the town and to the synagogue. Ezra would not presume to question any decision made by his patron, of course, but it all did seem extremely odd.

Just as it was time for James to go home, a figure appeared at the entrance to the synagogue court. Ezra rose at the sight of the visitor, a stout man with a silver gray beard who wore a brass badge suspended over his chest, marking him as a publican. This was someone Ezra knew well—too well, in fact—Eleazar, tax collector for the district.

"Peace be with you, Rabbi," the visitor said.

Ezra responded with measured politeness, "Peace be with you."

The look on Eleazar's face suggested that this call was a matter of business, not anything that touched on spiritual concerns or learned questions. But then, when the tax collector showed up it was always a matter of business, and generally unpleasant business at that. He and his ilk were referred to derisively as tax farmers. They bid on contracts from the Roman administration to collect the imperial levies within certain specified municipal areas. For their service they were given the right to add on their own charges. A common saying was that the only thing these farmers reaped was other people's money.

Eleazar held out a rolled-up piece of parchment tied with a ribbon and closed by an official-looking wax seal. "Rabbi," he said, "it is my duty to inform you that there will be an imperial census for the various jurisdictions of Palestine, by order of the Augustus. This document explains the details and the schedule. It is an official decree, which is to be read in the synagogue and then posted in a prominent place. All are to respond at the appointed time."

Ezra took the scroll and looked down at its seal. "I take it that Caesar is intending to favor us with new tax levies," he said.

"Caesar needs to know the scope of his realm and the number of people who dwell within it and depend on the security it affords," Eleazar pronounced imperiously. "We all enjoy that security, and we all must do our part to ensure it. Peace be with you, Rabbi." He turned and took his leave.

"What is happening?" James asked when the publican had gone.

Ezra tapped the scroll against the palm of his left hand. "We are being asked to give Caesar his due," the rabbi said, "or at least what he wishes to think is his due. What others think, we shall see."

Hearing about the census from James that evening, Joseph was perturbed. "New taxes," he said while seated at table in Josis' house. "This sort of thing inevitably brings trouble."

"Not without cause," Josis said. "Between the damnable charges for Herod's monstrous building projects, the temple tax, the head tax, and all the levies on property and crops, plus endless tolls and excises on anything transported and sold, people are bled dry."

"Herod built the temple," James observed innocently.

"And we never stop paying for it," said Josis.

Joseph sensed a fatherly need to step in. "Yes, James," he said. "The temple is Herod's crowning achievement. I myself, as someone who builds, can certainly appreciate its magnificent design and construction. But that project was a long and expensive undertaking. And while it can't be denied that the Holy One is properly honored by its grandeur, there are some who would call it a bit extravagant."

Josis tapped a finger emphatically on the table. "I do not think the Holy One would wish to see His people impoverished for the sake of a building," he said. "Any building."

"Well," said James rather weakly, "the temple is beautiful."

"When is this census to be held?" Joseph asked.

"The Rabbi Ezra said it would be around the Festival of Booths,"James replied. "Each man must travel to the place of his birth to register his household in the tally."

"I would expect that," said Joseph. "But at that time of year, roads are usually clogged with people on pilgrimage to Jerusalem—Jews and gentiles both. To schedule a census then? The holy days will be disrupted, crowding will be worse, the entire country will be upset."

"Our Roman lords take no concern for how people live," Salome interjected.

"At least there will be no traveling for us," Josis said. "We were all born here."

"You and your brothers," Joseph said. "But I will have to register in Bethlehem."

Josis looked across the table vacantly, then said, "You are right, Father. I did not think about that. And Bethlehem is so near Jerusalem."

"Another walk for me," Joseph said with a shrug.

But Josis looked serious. "You will need to take care, Father," he said. "If there is trouble over this census, it will likely be in the district of Jerusalem."

"Perhaps I can attach myself to a caravan," said Joseph. "Don't worry, I will be cautious."

"Where does Lucillus have to go, Father?" James asked. "He was not born here at all."

"Probably Caesarea," said Joseph. "That is where he received his manumission."

The meal proceeded with more talk of Romans and taxes and the inconvenience of a census. What was left unspoken was any reference to the previous day's family meeting or Mary's child. Yet the situation hung in the air, demanding careful choices in words. There were moments when conversation seemed a bit forced.

After the meal was finished, Joseph took his eldest son out into the court. "Josis, I have been considering something," he said.

"Yes, Father?"

"Would you object to moving your workshop, my son?"

"My workshop? To where?"

"To the front corner of the court. I can bring in some men, and we can build you a larger structure, right next to the gate."

"Fine, Father. But why?"

"Well..." said Joseph hesitantly, "it is of course...customary...for a bridegroom to build his bride a new house...or add to the house of his father if they are to live with the family. And since so much about my marriage to Mary is...not customary...I thought... Well, your shop adjoins my house, and I thought that...with Mary's child coming, I could convert that space..."

Josis sensed—what, embarrassment?—in the way his father was speaking. This was a clear indication of the prevailing discomfort. The eldest son gave a knowing smile and touched him affectionately on the shoulder.

"Anything you wish, Father," said Josis reassuringly. "A bigger shop would be very welcome."

CHAPTER NINE

TENSION AND ANOTHER DEPARTURE

All went to be enrolled, each to his own city,
and Joseph also went up from Galilee.
(Luke 2)

T he Sepphoris project that had demanded so much attention from Joseph and Lucillus was completed by early spring.

Many shared the opinion that this was one of the handsomest structures in the city—well proportioned and not overly ornamented—adding to the reputation of the Nazareth builder. The Greek owner had by now forgotten all about the irregularities of the beams and boasted of how shrewd he had been in negotiating an excellent price for the work.

"Now these Jews know whom they are dealing with," he told a friend.

For his part, Josis was relieved that he had not been called upon to act for his father again in this matter. He contented himself with getting his tools, equipment and supplies moved into the new, larger shop which Joseph's men had erected in the front corner of the court.

Joseph also had his crew fix up the space Josis had just vacated, in preparation for Mary's return. With his young wife's prospects now changed from a life of prayer and study to one of motherhood, Joseph and James would sleep in the upper room, leaving the added area on the lower level for Mary's use in caring for her baby. James was happy to have their old quarters restored.

Worry about the census and the new taxes it would surely bring was starting to be felt throughout all of Herod's territories. Even though the count was still several months away, there had already been stirrings of unrest. These mainly consisted of angry but poorly organized groups calling on the people to refuse participation. However, there were rumors that the Zealot faction, the network of secret bands known as dagger-men, intent on overthrowing the Roman occupation, had plans for disruptive strikes on the counting stations.

To both encourage public cooperation and dissuade any would-be attackers, the level of Roman force was increased. Auxiliaries were brought in from Syria to supplement the garrisons, and there was some transiting of units between posts, mainly for the sake of increased visibility on the roads. But these early adjustments were minor. Spring and summer would pass before the census became an immediate concern, plenty of time to implement any other security measures necessary. Meanwhile, the new planting season and the approach of Passover provided other matters to occupy the minds of the populace.

Within the walls of Joseph's compound, one particular

event claimed everyone's interest. Zipporah announced that she was with child again, the fourth for her and Simon. The effect of this news was mixed. It served to deflect attention from Mary, especially among the women. That was a source of relief for Joseph. At the same time, it underscored the contrast between the normal joy of family expectation and his wife's peculiar circumstance. He decided that, on balance, it helped the situation. And in any event, who could deny the blessing of a new grandchild?

Another point of anticipation for the family was the olive grove which Judas and Simon were developing. The earliest trees they had planted were finally of an age where the brothers expected their first decent crop, and they looked forward to this year's picking. Josis had promised his brothers that he would build them an olive press, and sitting prominently in his new shop were the timbers he intended to cut and shape for the framing.

James, of course, had his own milestone to look forward to. The celebration of his maturity would take place in the fall. Not only would this mark his full participation in the synagogue, if Zacharias lived up to his pledge, James would soon be sent to Jerusalem to study with some great doctor of the Law. His feelings about that swung between excitement and unease, since it would mean the end of childhood and the start of a new and very different life. But ambivalence was understandable in one facing such a turning point, even if still a few months away.

Joseph sensed his son's mood. To boost the boy's enthusiasm and divert him from his fears, he suggested that James and Lucillus begin planning for the day of James' reading in the synagogue. Not that the celebration should be too elaborate, Joseph cautioned. James agreed, but it did require some effort for him to keep a rein on his imagination.

The week after Passover, Joseph received a message from Mary. Elizabeth had given birth to a son, whom the parents named John. The courier, a guard of the temple, was provided with a meal, and his horse fed and watered while Joseph read Mary's note and prepared a response.

Mary asked if her husband preferred that she remain longer in Ein Kerem or if he desired her presence in Nazareth. Zacharias and Elizabeth, enthralled at the birth of their child—which, interestingly enough, had occurred on the very day of Passover itself—expressed their happiness at Mary remaining, if that was what Joseph thought best. Otherwise, transport would be secured for her. In closing, Mary noted that Zacharias had recovered his voice.

Joseph composed a note for the courier to take back to his wife. He wrote that he had explained her situation to the family. The reaction was what one would expect, and he believed all were doing their best to accept the truth of his account. He felt it would be helpful if she could return and work through any difficulties in having her received back into the household before she gave birth. And he noted that Zipporah was also with child, which might dispose the women toward greater sympathy for Mary's condition—at least that was his hope. Consequently, she should return to Nazareth as soon as it was convenient for her to do so. He would be most grateful if Zacharias could arrange for her safe conveyance.

Nearly three weeks passed before those arrangements came to fruition. Mary was reluctant to leave before Elizabeth had recovered fully from the delivery, which was somewhat hampered by her years. There was also a question about whether age would preclude the ability to nurse a child. Blessedly this proved no problem. Elizabeth's milk came in surprising abundance, and a wet nurse was not required.

Raised in the temple, Mary had never witnessed childbirth. Neither had she any knowledge of what was required in the care of a newborn. Elizabeth's experience proved a valuable opportunity for instruction before Mary would face her own motherhood, and she considered it a timely gift.

Mary's return was both unexpected and startling. Caravans regularly passed south of Nazareth, following the road that ran along the Jezreel Valley. But they rarely diverted up into the hill towns. Few could recall the last time a camel was seen in Nazareth streets. And so it was a novelty when one day a trio of the hulking beasts paraded by the synagogue and through the square.

The Rabbi Ezra was taken aback to see them lumbering along in their rocking, ship-like gait. The boys of the class, reacting to their teacher's wide-eyed visage, turned to watch the heads of the animals and their riders passing above the wall of the court. James was especially surprised to observe that the second camel in the train bore Mary.

He turned back to the rabbi. "It is my father's bride," said the boy. He stood, unthinking, as if to start for home, then stopped and looked at Ezra.

When word of Joseph's marriage had spread throughout the town, there was ample speculation about why the carpenter would leave his new wife with her relatives. The sudden, out-of-town wedding was extraordinary enough and certainly conducive to gossip. That Joseph would permit his young bride to be separated from him was beyond any sensible explanation.

Aware of this chatter, the Rabbi Ezra returned James' glance and nodded in the direction of the gate. "Perhaps you should go, James son of Joseph," he said. "Your father may need help getting his wife settled."

"Yes, Rabbi," said the boy.

He ran after the small caravan, past curious onlookers along the way, overtaking it at the edge of town. "Mary," he called.

She heard him, smiled down, and waved. "Peace be with you, James," she called from atop her swaying perch.

The train continued up the hill to the compound, drawing to a halt in front. James ran to the gate, touched the scroll quickly, and went inside. Josis, having heard the distinctive clanking of the camels' harness bells, emerged from his new shop, just within the walls.

"What is happening?" he asked.

"Mary is here," said James, running across the court to the portico past household children seeking out the sound. He found his father seated with Lucillus at the table inside the house, inspecting a set of building plans. "Father," he said, "Mary has arrived. She's on a camel."

"A camel?"

The two men rose and followed the boy out into the court and across to the gate. The children were already outside the wall, clustered around the big animals; their mothers close behind in a state of some concern. Words of caution were heard from the women.

The lead camel had lowered itself to the ground, its driver now standing beside the beast that carried Mary, motioning for it to sit as well. When it had settled, Mary swung a leg over the front horn of her saddle, the wooden frame of which bore a cushioned seat above the camel's hump. She held her robes tight to her legs for modesty, and climbed down, stepping over the packs that hung from the harness rigging.

Joseph stood before his bride. "Peace be with you, Mary," he said.

"Peace be with you, my husband," she responded.

He looked at the animals. "This is an unexpected mode of transport," he said, amused.

"Zacharias had me join a caravan headed for Tyre," Mary explained. "It is stopped awaiting the return of these men and their animals where the road from Nazareth meets the main highway to the seacoast. Then it will continue on."

The lead driver had detached two large bundles from the harness and brought them around to Mary. "Your possessions, Mistress," he said.

"Thank you for your care and your kindness," Mary said. "Please convey my gratitude to Master Zacharias."

Lucillus reached into the scrip he carried on his belt and took out two coins, which he gave to the driver for himself and his companion.

The man received the gratuity with a bow. "May the blessings of the Holy One be upon the house of Joseph," he said. Then he remounted his camel, signaled the beasts to rise, and the train set off back through town.

Josis and Lucillus each picked up one of Mary's bundles and carried them inside the compound as the children watched the camels disappear down the road. The wives each shot a quick glance at Mary's front, curious if any sign of her condition might show on her small frame.

Aware of their interest, Mary nodded to each woman in turn. "Sarah, Zipporah, Salome," she said, "peace be upon you all. It is good to see you again."

Each nodded coolly in response.

Josis and Lucillus had deposited the bundles in the main room by the table and departed when Mary and Joseph came in. Alone now, Joseph inquired as to his wife's wellbeing.

"I am very fine, husband," she said.

"The trip was not too difficult?"

"I found that riding on the cushioned saddle of a camel is more comfortable than on a donkey's back," she said. "It is softer. But you must hold on tightly against the swaying."

"And the child?"

"All seems well. I look forward to feeling him move. Elizabeth says it should happen within a few weeks."

Joseph showed her the added room—she had, of course, noted Josis' new shop in the court. As Mary inspected the converted space, Joseph cautioned her about the tension that permeated the household.

"I know that everyone wishes to believe what I told them," he said. "At least, they want to believe that I am not mad or that you have not bewitched me. But their willingness to accept you and the child remains to be seen. It is difficult for them, as I'm sure you realize."

"We ask them to accept what seems a blasphemy," Mary said.

"Yes," Joseph said, hands turned up in a gesture of resignation. "I understand their feelings. It is how I first reacted. And I realize that they will need time. They have received no messages of confirmation as I did. Meanwhile, things may be awkward for you."

She offered her husband a gentle smile. "The Lord is my rock, my fortress, my deliverer, my God, my strength, in whom I take refuge."

Then they spoke of Mary's sojourn in Ein Kerem, of Elizabeth's delivery, and the naming of the child.

"Elizabeth had insisted he be called John," she said. "Everyone wondered why, since there is no one named John in the family. But Zacharias wrote on his tablet that he agreed the child was to be called John. It was very strange, my husband. At that moment he regained his voice."

Joseph shook his head. Just one more odd occurrence to ponder in all of this.

Mary shared an experience of which she was quite proud. She had learned to make the Sabbath bread.

"While Elizabeth was recovering from her delivery, I spent time with the servants in the kitchen," she said. "I must admit I had to be a bit evasive about it. My aunt would have been horrified if she knew I did household work there. Even when she herself was laid low, she kept trying to fuss over me. But I wanted to learn, so I swore everyone to secrecy." She laughed at the memory, then looked at Joseph. "Was that wrong, my husband?"

Joseph shook his head. "I think the deception was done lovingly," he said.

"Maybe I can demonstrate my bread-making to Salome," Mary said. "She was teaching me to cook before I went away. She might be pleased."

"Perhaps," Joseph said with something less than certainty.

Over the next few days Mary made tentative gestures toward each of the wives. She offered congratulations to Zipporah for the child who was to come. Zipporah received her words with a terse "Thank you," saying nothing about Mary's own state. Likewise, the blandest of pleasantries were exchanged with Sarah when Mary joined Joseph and James at her table for the evening meal. Her husband, Judas, tried to be more forthcoming. But he, too, was affected by the awkwardness of the evening, and focused his conversation almost exclusively on this year's anticipated olive crop.

Salome's first response to Mary's report of making the Sabbath bread was little more than a grunt. Then, seeing sincerity in the girl's face, she reproached herself for dismissing this accomplishment—quite obviously something Mary had considered an important bit of progress. She put forth the effort to make her own expression more pleasant.

"That is good," she said.

Mary, standing with head slightly down, turned her eyes hesitantly toward Salome. "Perhaps I could...help you...at Sabbath...this week?" she asked.

Salome eyed her back—this mere slip of a girl who so absurdly was her mother-in-law. Mary was indeed a child, the same child she had been before, sheltered, wide-eyed, well-intentioned, naive. Could she really have sinned? It didn't seem possible. Yet there was Joseph's admission, her hasty departure. The explanation he had given couldn't be true.

Could it?

"Come early on the morning of preparation," she said, turning away. "We will bake."

Mary stood quietly for a moment, the shadow of a smile washing across her face. Then she returned to her house.

As weeks passed and spring became summer, feelings about the census continued to harden. Concern no longer centered only on the likelihood of new taxes, though that was always a prospect capable of stoking resentment. Certain rabbis raised religious questions, noting how David's decision to conduct a similar count, with the aim of raising an army, had brought suffering to the people.

One scholar voiced his objections right in the temple. Speaking to a crowd that had gathered in the Court of the Gentiles, he shouted, "Only the Holy One Himself has the right to number the people."

His listeners took up the point, chanting it over and over with increasing volume and emotional fervor. Eventually, temple guards were summoned to disperse the gathering.

Word of the incident made its way to Nazareth, raising the level of anxiety which Joseph's family felt about his impending trip to Bethlehem. News that additional Roman troops were being sent to police the census added to the fear, since a heightened military presence was as likely to provoke violence as suppress it. And all too often, when Romans took action, they showed little regard for the safety of innocent bystanders.

Joseph promised to find other men who would be traveling to register at towns around Jerusalem. He would be conscious of safety and not attempt the trip alone. This was as much reassurance as he could offer.

In truth, he didn't know how many would have to make the trek in that direction, Nazareth not being someplace to which very many people moved from other areas. He had settled here himself only because of the promise of opportunity in nearby Sepphoris and the willingness of old Avram's widow to sell her property at an especially attractive price. But he asked Lucillus to inquire around.

Meanwhile, James took to perusing passages of scripture for his day of reading in the synagogue. He wanted to find a Torah portion that was special, something to which he could bring a fresh thought. The Rabbi Ezra offered several suggestions, none of which seemed quite right to the boy.

Then James remembered the talk he and the rabbi shared about Cain and Abel. The story stuck in his mind, perhaps because of his own brothers. But there was something else. It was Ezra's observation that the Holy One had his own reasons for accepting Abel's offering and rejecting Cain's, reasons not made explicit in the Scriptural account.

Later in the story Cain is banished for killing Abel, but he is not slain as one would expect of a murderer. Cain actually is given a mark that is meant to protect him. Did this treatment also suggest a higher purpose, inexplicable as it might be? Cain did go on to beget a line of descendants. He even built a city—a fact that was of mild interest, since James' own father was a builder.

The lesson seemed to lie in the unexpected way in which the Lord's will was worked out. Even a man who had done something as wicked as murdering his brother could still serve the Holy One's purpose. It was an intriguing idea and, James decided, one worth exploring. Ezra agreed, and he suggested some writings on which the boy might draw for his commentary.

A rumor began to spread that the Zealots now considered cooperating in the census a betrayal of the nation. No one could say for sure if there would be violent reprisals against individuals, but worry about the possibility was growing. Walking parties were organized for those traversing long distances. The organizers secured documents of passage from the Roman authorities so they would not be mistaken for protestors. In some cases, arrangements were made for armed soldiers to provide security, since troublemakers might infiltrate the groups.

Through his inquiries, Lucillus learned of one party coming from the coast through the Jezreel Valley. It would stop at towns and villages along the way to take on additional travelers, the better to ensure safety for all. Joseph could join it where the road from Nazareth connected.

Lucillus found a similar party bound for Caesarea, and planned to travel with it himself.

It was clear that the impact of the census would be significant well beyond any simple inconvenience it imposed on daily life. The harvest would be complicated tremendously, since crops would have to be brought in and all threshing completed before the loss of field hands who might have to be counted in other places. Trade would come virtually to a standstill, with the roads clogged and many draft and pack animals diverted to the moving of people rather than the transporting of goods.

Joseph and Lucillus determined that disruption of work on their current projects would be minimal, most of the crewmen being locally born. But getting supplies would be a problem during the count and the weeks before and after. Joseph was especially concerned about a consignment of stone scheduled for delivery during that period. When the material might actually arrive was now impossible to say, though he thought it predictable that there would be another unhappy client.

With all his inquiries, Lucillus became aware of certain whisperings among the people in town. That Mary carried a child had apparently become known beyond the family compound, even though she hadn't set foot outside its walls since her return from Ein Kerem. The blooming of a fertile young wife, even one with a much older husband, was hardly surprising, but some noted that no announcement had been made in the synagogue.

Joseph's prediction that people would calculate was thoroughly borne out as speculation spread. Imaginings about the size of Mary's belly—which some people maintained, on the best of authority, was gigantic—validated the concern Joachim had expressed about the viciousness of Nazareth gossip.

Lucillus dutifully, if reluctantly, reported what he learned to Joseph, who worried what effect this talk might have on the household. It didn't take long to find out. Sarah came to him in an agitated state to complain of some particularly nasty comments overheard in the market street.

"This bodes ill for the whole family," she said with consternation. "You must do something, Father."

He received similar reports, and a similar plea, from both of his daughters, Lydia and Assia. Simon weighed in as well, even though Judas had cautioned against burdening their father with idle gossip. And those who didn't come forth with such stories were now conducting themselves with a disquieting reserve. All chose their words with the utmost care whenever Mary was present, and avoided mentioning her name to Joseph when she was not.

Finally a remark, uttered outside the synagogue after the morning service, came to Joseph's ears directly. The speaker stopped in mid-sentence when he realized that Joseph was still within hearing distance.

But Joseph didn't need the concluding words to make clear what was implied. His family had never before been touched by any sort of scandal, and yet people were indulging such foul thoughts. But if they wanted to talk, who could stop them? Joseph's concern was for the peace of his household, which he sensed was slipping away.

Surely he couldn't have been wrong in agreeing to take Mary. The divine origin of her child, the revelation by the Lord's messenger, the son of Zacharias and Elizabeth, given to them so late in life, as Mary herself had been given to Joachim and Anna—all of these things and more pointed to some greater design. For reasons known only to the Holy One, Joseph's family had been chosen to carry out a mission whose purpose and scope remained yet unclear.

It would not be easy. With this mission came risk. Hadn't the prophets been brought to strife in the Lord's service? How could Joseph not be surprised that his sons and their wives and his daughters and their husbands were so distressed? He had asked them to accept a claim that any righteous Jew—or any intelligent person, for that matter—

would find improbable at best and, at worst, a damnable lie. They were all good, faithful people, not without their faults but sound at the core. That was their great strength and the strength of the family. But Joseph realized this was also what would make it hard for them ever to accept Mary and her child. And here was where the risk lay.

If his kin could not accept, then surely the townspeople, so quick to revel in their base conjecturing, might assume anything vile. How could the family not be touched by that? And what if a serious charge were to be leveled against his wife? Could they be counted upon to stand together in firm defense of her name when their own conviction was so lacking?

Perhaps he should have had her remain in Ein Kerem. People would have wondered why she stayed away, true, but they might not have found out she carried a child. Which might have made it easier on the family, better allowing feelings to be calmed and reservations to ease.

These thoughts weighed heavily on Joseph's mind as the time of the census drew near—and the time for Mary to deliver. What could he do? He was required to be in Bethlehem for the count, and he could barely think of bringing her along, heavy with child. Still, painful as it was to admit, he did not feel confident leaving Mary with his family. Never before had he wanted for trust in his own children. But he had to face his feelings.

Not unexpectedly, it was Zipporah who forced a difficult but unavoidable decision.

Occupying the lower level of the house, Mary had taken to reciting her prayers outside in the portico, especially when Joseph and Lucillus were discussing building projects at the table, as was their habit. Mary prayed with intense concentration, totally absorbed, the upper part of her body rocking forward and back, forward and back without her even being aware of the motion.

While she positioned herself discreetly by the large bush that grew at the corner of the portico, Mary was still visible. All the adults in the family had observed her in this attitude, each pondering to some degree the question of whether it was appropriate for a woman to be seen praying in such a manner—that is, like a man—even within the confines of the household.

Zipporah's reaction was more visceral. The sight of Mary's now large and protrusive belly seemed to her a stark contrast with the piety represented by the shuckling movements. The holy temple girl with child, and such a wild story given as explanation—it could only be regarded as hypocrisy in the extreme, and it made Zipporah feel actually ill. She shared her opinion with Salome one afternoon as they came in the front gate after a trip to the market street.

The older woman was torn. "You should not let such feelings take hold of you so," she said. "It does good neither for you, nor for the family. I know it's hard to accept what Father Joseph told us. But Mary seems such an honest and innocent girl. And who can say what the Holy One might do?"

Zipporah's laugh in response was tinged with cynicism. "You have a good heart, Salome," she said, "and so you take Mary under your wing. You want to believe. But tell me honestly, do you really think this story can be true?"

Salome hesitated. "I don't... I don't...know," she said.

Joseph happened to be inside the new carpentry shop with Josis. The words of his daughters-in-law passed easily through the open doorway and the light wooden planking of the walls. He glanced at his eldest son, whom he realized had also overheard. Josis concentrated intently on his work.

Lucillus and Josis both tried to talk Joseph out of taking Mary on the journey. After the painful incident of the conversation between his and Simon's wives, Josis was particularly eager to reassure his father that Mary would be safest at home.

"She will need the women, especially if she delivers before your return," he insisted earnestly. "I understand that feelings are strained. But Father, you must realize no one would leave Mary uncared for. She is your wife."

"Travel would be an ordeal for one in her condition," Lucillus added in support. "Please reconsider."

But Joseph was adamant. He would take Mary to Bethlehem, register for the census, and then go on to Ein Kerem. Bringing her back to Nazareth had been a mistake. Given the miraculous nature of all that had happened, Zacharias and Elizabeth would be happy to have her. They were convinced there was a connection between the birth of their son and the coming of Mary's child. Joseph was inclined to that view himself. Perhaps he would leave her there indefinitely. He would still be her husband, providing her with any necessary legal rights and protections. But maybe the Holy One intended for the two children to be raised together.

And so it was that Joseph and Mary departed from the family compound with Lucillus on the morning after the last Sabbath before the Festival of Booths. Mary was perched uncomfortably on the back of Lucillus' donkey. The Greek accompanied them down to where the road from Nazareth connected with the highway in the Jezreel Valley.

There Lucillus continued toward the west to meet the walking party headed down the coast to Caesarea. Joseph and Mary awaited their party bound for the district of Jerusalem.

Several steps along, Lucillus paused for a moment and turned back for a farewell wave. He experienced a shiver of anxiety. But then he willed himself to smile, and continued on his way.

CHAPTER TEN
REVELATION AND ESCAPE

He took the young Child and His mother by night
and departed for Egypt.
(Matthew 2)

After the months of tension, there was a definite sense of relief among the adults in the family—accompanied by a degree of guilt for feeling it—when Joseph and Mary departed for Bethlehem. But this soon gave way to fascination with an unusual effect that appeared in the sky. Each night for several weeks an especially bright star would rise in the east and appear to pause at a point in the general direction of Jerusalem, until finally it would disappear in the light of dawn.

The phenomenon drew attention throughout the country, and was remarked upon widely as something quite unlike anything ever noted within common memory. But eventually, the prominence of the star faded, and the sky returned to its normal appearance. Thoughts among the family members drifted back to the unresolved conflict over Mary. There was also some concern about what Joseph's attitude would be when he returned without her. He did not return, however. Nothing was heard of him for many weeks.

Even with a side trip to Ein Kerem after registering for the census at Bethlehem, Joseph should have been back long ago. Lucillus, who returned from Caesarea within days of his own registration, used his extensive contacts to seek out people who had been in the walking party with Joseph and Mary. He found several. One reported that the pair had stood in line with him waiting to be counted in Bethlehem. Nobody knew anything of their whereabouts afterward.

All in the family were worried, some harboring secret fears of the worst kind. Though the strong presence of Roman troops did succeed in keeping the anticipated troubles to a minimum, a few serious clashes had occurred. Predictably, these had gotten blown up into rumors of copious blood spilt, though it was unclear exactly how many attacks, how many casualties, and whether ordinary citizens were involved. Not all the rumors told of political acts. There were also stories of brigands pouncing on travelers who ventured into secluded paths or those unwise enough to attempt the trip unaccompanied.

For James, Joseph's unexplained absence not only held anxiety, it brought a particular disappointment. Celebration of the boy's maturity had been set for five weeks after the Festival of Booths. That day came and went. Lucillus cancelled the great fest they had planned, and called upon all the invited guests, informing them that a new date would be announced when Joseph returned. Meanwhile, the

Rabbi Ezra asked James if he wanted to go ahead and read without the celebration, but the boy insisted his father should be present.

James was crestfallen and deeply worried. Joseph would never miss such an important event unless something serious had happened. It was the first time James had come face to face with the threats contained in life's uncertainty, and he was shaken by the experience. Sensing his brother's distress, Josis invited James to sleep in his house. But James declined. Even if he hadn't yet done his first reading, he was a man now, and a man had to take care of himself.

Josis put his hand on James' shoulder and gave a nod of respect. "That is true, Brother," he said understandingly. "Still...if you should need anything..."

James looked up into his eldest brother's eyes, paused and, speaking unsteadily, said, "Yes... I will..." Then, after a moment: "Do you think Father and Mary are... Do you think they're alright?"

"I don't know," Josis said. "We must pray for their protection."

Another rumor had begun making the rounds, a story that was inexplicable, if not outright bizarre, and yet maintained as true by a variety of seemingly reliable sources. It was said that Herod's minions were scouring the town of Bethlehem for male children, from newly born to two years of age.

As with most rumors, several versions circulated, the most benign of which described palace officials checking circumcision records and interrogating parents in a sort of follow-up to the census. The most horrific variant told of soldiers actually killing children, often right in front of parents forcibly restrained and wailing in grief and madness.

It would have been easy to dismiss the wildest of the tales as utter nonsense, except for the king's reputation as a scheming and heartless brute. Hadn't he killed members of his own family? It was Caesar himself who commented, "Better to be Herod's pig than his son." Those words became a joke when someone noted that dietary laws would hardly restrain the only-nominally Jewish Herod. "Perhaps the pig really would not be so much better off, after all" went the saying. "At least Herod's sons aren't likely to be eaten."

The significance of Bethlehem as the focus of these rumors was not lost on James when a classmate related the story about the children to him. In a panic the boy ran home, bursting through the gate without touching the scroll, and startling Josis in his workshop.

"Calm yourself," Josis said in response to James' rushed and frantic report. "Yes, I heard something about the king's soldiers looking for children. I don't know why they are doing it, or even if it is true."

"But my friend told me it happened in Bethlehem," James said breathlessly. "Father and Mary are in Bethlehem, and Mary carries a child."

"We don't know that they are still in Bethlehem. Father planned on going from there to Ein Kerem. Perhaps they are at the house of Zacharias. Or they could be anywhere."

After a few agitated minutes, Josis succeeded in getting James settled down. He promised the boy he would try to find out whatever he could, and Lucillus would as well. In the meantime, they must all be patient and continue to pray until some word came from their father.

The truth was, however, that others in the family had also heard tales of missing or dead children in Bethlehem. James was not alone in his anxiety. The deeper Josis and Lucillus inquired into the matter, the more it seemed that something strange had indeed happened, though the bits of information they gleaned were second-hand and varied widely. Confirmation came in a frightening way on the day of preparation for Sabbath. Early in the morning there was a loud and violent pounding on the gate, setting the dogs to barking.

"Open for the king's officer!" called a harsh, insistent voice as morning light broke over the compound.

Simon emerged from his house, hastily arranging his tunic, and opened the gate. There was a squad of six armed soldiers bearing shields of the Royal Guard. Their captain stood in front.

"We seek Joseph son of Jacob," said the officer. "This is his home."

"Yes," said Simon.

"Who are you?"

"I am Simon. Joseph is my father."

Other family members had come out of their houses. Zipporah stood in her doorway, three bleary-eyed children around her.

"Where is your father?"

"We do not know."

"You don't know?"

"He went to register for the census, and he has not returned. We have heard nothing from him."

"He registered in Bethlehem."

"Well, he was going to—"

"He did. We know this." The captain's eyes swept the court. "Your father has a young wife."

"Yes. Mary, daughter of Joachim."

"She was with him at the count."

Simon shrugged.

"She was. They were seen. And she has delivered a child."

"We did not know that. She still carried the child when they left."

Josis and Judas had come to the gate and were standing behind Simon. Their wives stood by their doors. Sarah held one of her children in her arms. James was in the portico.

"Your father's wife has given birth," said the captain. "We know that this happened at a lodging in Bethlehem."

"When?"

"Just after the Festival of Booths. It was a boy. His name is Jesus."

"Jesus?"

The officer looked at Simon, then at Josis and Judas. "This family is curiously ignorant of its father's movements."

"As my brother told you," said Josis, "we have had no word."

The officer grunted. Then he gestured to the soldiers, and they passed through the gate by the three brothers. "We will inspect the household," the officer said. "You will cooperate."

The squad dispersed throughout the compound. Solders went into each of the houses. Sarah and Salome each followed after as they entered. The crying of a frightened child was heard from Judas' house. Sarah emerged again with a second child in her arms.

One of the soldiers, who appeared to be the captain's subaltern, whispered something in his superior's ear. Then he pointed toward Zipporah, who reacted with a start. Simon looked anxiously at his wife.

"No," said the captain to his man. "The child we seek has been born."

Zipporah's hands went instinctively to her belly.

"There are no children in this household under the age of two years?" the captain asked of anyone who would reply.

"None," said Josis.

The officer eyed him up and down. "You are..."

"I am Josis, eldest brother of the family."

The captain opened his hand, and the subaltern placed a sheet of parchment into it. The captain scanned the writing, then looked back up at Josis, saying only, "Yes."

Silence followed. The brothers stood awkwardly, nervously, unsure of what would happen next and knowing that whatever did happen, they would be powerless to do anything about it. The soldiers completed their search of the buildings in the compound and returned to the gate. One of them said, "They are not here, sir."

The captain gestured; his men went out into the street. He looked at Josis again but said nothing. Then he turned and left.

Zipporah sank down onto the threshold of the doorway. Her body was suddenly taken over by a violent trembling she could not control. Simon rushed to his wife, kneeling down and taking her in his arms.

She looked up into his eyes, began to speak, hesitated, then said, "Mary. It's true."

Several days later, Lucillus came to Josis in his workshop. "I was visited early this morning by Lemuel, the steward of Zacharias," he said in hushed tones.

Josis put down the mallet and chisel with which he was working and looked intently into Lucillus' eyes. "What of Father?"

"He is in Egypt," Lucillus said.

"Egypt?"

"Zacharias waited until Joseph could get Mary and the baby out of the country before sending a message. The child Herod seeks is hers, though he probably does not know it. Lemuel said that Joseph wishes us to keep all the projects going and to continue operating the business. On no account should anyone in the family do anything that suggests we know where he is. He will contact us when he feels it is safe. Also, he sends his apology to James and instructs him to go ahead with his reading in the synagogue."

The two men looked at each other, the deepest gravity in both their expressions. This message could only mean that the family would not see Joseph and Mary for a long time.

AUTHOR'S NOTE

This book is a work of speculative fiction, based on incidents in the New Testament, re-imagined and elaborated on extensively. I have not attempted to create a "fifth gospel." Rather, I've tried to fill in some of the gaps between facts given in Scripture with inventive suppositions about *how things might have been.*

The Holy Bible is the most durable and influential book in the history of the world (a compendium of books, really). Yet anyone who reads it objectively must admit that the portrait it offers of life in Christ's time is often painted in broad strokes with little historical perspective or everyday detail.

Many of the situations presented in my story are suggested by the non-canonical writings of the early Christian period. These are the "gospels" and "testaments" that didn't make it into the Bible. Yet they reflect beliefs and traditions maintained by communities of people who identified themselves as followers of Christ.

Some of these traditions have resonance in Church practice to this day. For instance, a feast still found on the liturgical calendar, *The Presentation of the Blessed Virgin Mary in the Temple* (celebrated by both Catholics and Orthodox on November 21), is assumed by some scholars to reflect a tradition that Mary was raised in the temple at Jerusalem. Likewise, a view held primarily among Eastern Christians is that Joseph was considerably older than Mary, a widower with children, when they married. That idea is not disputed by Catholic dogma, and even some Protestants find that it sheds light on many questions about the relationship between Mary and Joseph (and about what Catholics and Orthodox maintain on the subject) that otherwise go unanswered by Scripture.

In addition to the non-canonical works, I drew on many other print and online sources, most of which cite two authors whose accounts figure prominently in virtually all histories of the period: the Jewish general-turned-historian, Flavius Josephus (c. 37-100 C.E.), and Eusebius, Bishop of Caesarea (c. 260-339 C.E.), who compiled an account of the Church's first three centuries.

Pulling all of these various informational threads together and weaving them into a story presented some challenges which I was able to confront only by taking a good deal of creative license. But I have hewn to one central commitment, that *I would not contradict the Bible*. Extract from it selectively? Yes. Adapt and embroider? Most elaborately. And, to be sure, do a bit of hedging now and then to bridge the variations between different Gospel accounts. But not contradict.

For instance, I have described the principal circumstances of Jesus' birth largely as traditionally told (except for the date of Christmas), despite the fact that scholars have long struggled with a conflict between that event and the time of the great census which the Bible tells us found Joseph and Mary in Bethlehem. The discrepancy between the Gospel accounts and other documentary evidence of the period is as much as ten years. I also had to address variations with which the four evangelist/authors of the Gospels list events in Jesus' ministry. I mainly followed the order given in the Book of Luke while including some episodes mentioned by the other Gospel writers.

In order to move my plot along, making the things happen that I wanted to have happen at times that seemed to make the most sense, I have taken a loose approach to *sequence* and *duration*. Biblical incidents are referenced with some arbitrariness on my part. And while the major non-Scriptural historical events cited in my story are real, I have reconfigured them freely and either compressed, extended or shifted the time in which it is believed they occurred. Naturally, most of the narrative details are imagined, since two thousand years later, there's no way of knowing exactly how events unfolded.

But then, this is a novel, not a historical treatise or catechetical tract.

No doubt there are many points in the book which can be debated, and I've likely gotten some details wrong. But my goal has been to tell a plausible story about human beings confronting an extraordinary situation—indeed the most extraordinary situation imaginable: *God present in human form*. I wanted to explore how different individuals (both historical figures and made-up characters) might have behaved, presenting motives and feelings that would ring true to readers today.

Because, despite the passage of twenty centuries and the differences in cultural context, human nature is consistent. The people of Jesus' era really were very much like us. In particular, I felt it was important to paint a detailed picture of the political currents in First-Century

Palestine, especially as they affected reactions to Jesus and his movement.

It's easy to get a shallow, Sunday-school impression that the Jews of Christ's time were a bunch of thin-skinned spoilsports, very confused about what was really important. Why would anybody want to kill someone who went around preaching love and offering a lot of uplifting homilies? And healing the sick to boot! Well, there were reasons why Jesus was seen as a threat, and I have attempted to suggest some of them.

It has been my experience that people often need *a way* to think about religious ideas and questions of faith. While the Bible speaks with profundity on all the great themes of human existence and has an indisputable track record for changing lives, it very often raises as many questions as it answers. That's why well-organized, scholarly Scripture study, conducted within an informed historical context, is a critical component of effective religious education.

In my story I have tried to offer a way to think about the great events that befell the Holy Family, most particularly James, whom the Bible names as head of the Church in Jerusalem and calls *the brother of the Lord*. I would not begin to claim that all my suppositions are correct. But I do claim a certain kind of inspiration in coming up with them—surely not of the caliber experienced by the Gospel writers, but sufficient to keep me going whenever the well of creativity seemed to have run dry. I offer a sincere prayer of thanks for that, gratefully acknowledging His help and guidance.

Bill Kassel

ABOUT THE AUTHOR

BILL KASSEL has made a specialty of conveying religious ideas and moral precepts in accessible ways to a broad public.  He produces and hosts a weekly radio series, "Free Expression," featuring talks with key authors and religious communicators, distributed by Michigan EWTN-affiliate, Good Shepherd Catholic Radio.

During the 1980s, he founded and led a popular Catholic music ensemble called Company, which was a forerunner of today's Independent Catholic Music Movement. He is a songwriter, Christian entertainer, and essayist, and has authored two Christian mysteries, *Holy Innocents* (2000) and *This Side of Jordan* (2003), along with his award-winning historical novel, *My Brother's Keeper*.

Kassel created and hosted a series of religious comedy programs, called *Kassel & Company*, for Ave Maria Radio, the national Catholic programming service. He also produced a 90-minute music special that spotlighted rising independent Catholic artists. And he has released an album of his own original Christian songs, titled *On This Mountain*.

A writer whose career has been highly varied, Kassel

has been a journalist, advertising copywriter, and public relations consultant. He's held creative staff positions with such prestigious companies as Dow Jones and McGraw-Hill. He was also director of public affairs for Hillsdale College, and director of communications for The Ave Maria Foundation.

Writing under his own byline or as a ghostwriter for others, he has authored or edited non-fiction books as well as articles appearing in *The Wall Street Journal*, *The New York Times*, *Los Angeles Times*, *Chicago Tribune*, *USA Today*, *Newsweek*, *National Catholic Register*, *American Thinker*, *Aleteia*, *New Oxford Review*, and numerous other publications and online journals.

Kassel is married with two grown children. He and his wife, Kathleen, reside in Michigan. His thoughts and random rants can be found at his blog, *The Guy in the Next Pew* (www.billkassel.com).

NOVELS BY BILL KASSEL

Holy Innocents

My Brother's Keeper

This Side of Jordan

www.ingramcontent.com/pod-product-compliance
Lightning Source LLC
Chambersburg PA
CBHW020637110726
47899CB00002B/796